CW01456778

THE COWBOY'S SOULMATE
COURAGE COUNTY BRIDES

MIA BRODY

This is a work of fiction. Names, characters, places, and incidents either are the product of the author's imagination or are used fictitiously. Any resemblance to actual persons, living or dead, events, or locales is entirely coincidental.

Copyright © 2022 by Mia Brody

All rights reserved. No part of this book may be reproduced or used in any manner without written permission of the author except for the use of quotations in a book review.

1
LOGAN

"This is how you're choosing to spend your last night of freedom?" Archer, my brother, mocks me.

We're sitting together at the top of the Courage County water tower that overlooks the whole town. It's a damn cold place to be in the middle of January, but we've been coming up here to drink together since we were in high school. "I thought we'd be out at the bar and finding some women to take home."

It's a fair statement. In years past, that's exactly what I would have done. Except my boots haven't been under a woman's bed in a couple of years. Not that you would know that by the way the good ole gossip mill keeps churning.

"It's his bachelor party. Shut up," Ethan, my other

brother, says. He drops his beer and I listen for the sound of it hitting the dumpster below.

When the glass finally breaks, I let out a breath I didn't even realize I'd been holding. Tomorrow, I'm getting hitched to a woman I barely know. A mail-order bride that I've never even laid eyes on. All I got about her was a profile with some general information. Same as her.

Marriage has never been on my radar. It's just another way to tie yourself to someone who will up and leave you one day. I learned as a foster kid, it's better to be the one that does the leaving. Goodbye doesn't hurt so much when you say it first.

But my grandfather, God rest his soul, was a romantic. He had decades of wedded bliss and wanted to share this *gift* with his eight foster grand-kids. So, the old man strong-armed us into this upon his passing. In order to inherit any portion of the ranch, every Scott man must marry. Old coot even went so far as to choose a mail-order bride service for us.

"The whole town is betting against you," Archer warns. Out of all my brothers, he's the blunt one. He never holds in anything he's thinking or feeling. Yet somehow, the man is a millionaire.

He came up with some innovative design for

tractors in high school and patented it. Now he's an idea man, travels all over the globe, and consults with companies for millions of dollars. You'd think that would make him stuck up. But to hear Archer tell it, he still puts on his Wranglers same as everyone else. One leg at a time.

The knowledge the town is betting against me isn't surprising. In high school, I started sleeping around and got a reputation as the playboy. Can't say I've ever cared too much what people think so I didn't pay attention to the rumors. But over the years, the reputation has followed me. Now, I can't talk to a woman in town without tongues wagging.

"Everyone says you'll cheat on her within the first three months," Archer continues.

I've never cheated on a woman. Yeah, there have been more than a few in my life. But it never overlapped, and I was careful not to make promises I had no intention of keeping. To me, it was all good times until two years ago when it stopped being fun.

I don't know what exactly changed. All I know is that the games got old and the chase got boring. I was craving something else though I still can't tell you to this day what that something else is. *Guess I'll never figure it out now.*

Ethan smacks the back of Archer's head, and I

take a sip of my beer to hide my grin. Archer will say anything on his mind while Ethan barely speaks at all.

"What do you reckon she's going to look like?" Archer asks, shooting a scowl Ethan's way. He scoots just far enough to be out of reach of our serious, older brother.

"Don't know," I grunt. I haven't let myself spend too much time thinking on this. The way I see it, there's not much point. After all, I spent hours building up the family for my new foster home. The social worker had talked them up and for the first time in a long-time, I was hopeful. I was old at that point. Thirteen, which is pretty much a death sentence in the system. Everyone wants the cute little babies who are still sweet and innocent. Nobody wants the big teenage boy who has a history of doing what it takes to survive.

But one look at the parents who got me, and I realized real quick there had been a mix-up. Their whispered conversation in another room wasn't hard to overhear. They'd been wanting a cute little six-year-old boy, not the six-foot one teenager.

Now I can't help wondering if this mail-order bride thing is going to be that all over again. She'll take one look at me and be disappointed that I'm not everything she hoped for. I'll be out on my ass in the rain.

"The important thing is to stay focused." Ethan accepts it when Archer passes us fresh beers. "You get your portion of the land."

Without each brother doing his part to save the Scott ranch, pieces of it will be sold at auction. Everyone knows the land is worth a premium on our side of the county, and there would be a lot of people eager to snap it up.

"I'll do my part and get hitched," I promise Ethan as I clink my beer to his.

Like me, all the Scott brothers were adopted by the late Scotts. But somewhere along the way, the rag-tag eight of us formed a brotherhood. One that's solid and enduring. *No matter what it takes, I won't fail them.*

Audrey

"I KNOW IT'S BEEN HARD. BUT I NEED YOU TO BE brave for a few more minutes," I tell Paisley Jolene as I wipe the formula from her face. She's just finished her afternoon feeding.

The six-month-old baby girl finally started to put on some weight last month. We'd moved into our first apartment together and it felt like things were falling into place for us. Until the rug got ripped out from underneath our feet.

I take a deep breath and push back the memories. I don't want to think about that night or the way it makes me feel. What matters now is that Paisley and I are safe. Or at least, I think we will be in this place.

Glancing around the Courage County Bus Station, I'm glad we arrived a few minutes earlier than expected. It gave me time to feed Paisley and get her calm. As it is, my cowboy husband-to-be will show up with no idea that there's a baby on my hip.

I don't know what he'll do when he realizes he got a package deal. Maybe he'll send us away. The idea has my mouth going dry.

You don't become a mail-order bride at eighteen with a baby because your life is filled with options. I had to find a way to keep Paisley fed and safe. Moving to a small, rural town where no one knew us seemed like a good start.

My only hope is that the cops haven't tracked us this far. Then I remind myself that I've been on my own since I was fourteen. No one has missed me in four years. Why would someone start looking for me now?

As soon as I think that, an image of Calvin flashes in my mind. There was so much blood that night. He couldn't have survived, right?

Paisley pats my face as if she's reassuring me that the man who haunts my nightmares is truly gone. Then she gives me a grin, showing off that one little bottom tooth.

Even if I mess everything else up in my life, I know I did one thing right. I made Paisley, and this little girl needs her mama to be strong. She needs to know that unlike me, she always has a safe place to land.

Squaring my shoulders, I move to the bathroom to adjust my dark hair. It looks messy and oily thanks to the nearly thirty-hour bus ride. My groom offered a ticket on a plane or a bus.

I took the bus. I figured people were less likely to pay attention to us that way. So far, so good.

I scoop my messy hair into a ponytail and pause to pull a few tendrils loose to frame my face. Not that it does much. You can't soften the look of a woman who's spent as much time on the streets as I have.

Tugging on my short jean skirt, I wish it were

longer. But leaving the apartment in the middle of the night with nothing but the clothes on our backs has meant that I've been scraping by on whatever I could find in those donation bins down in Miami. That explains the red, sparkly tank top that's about a size too small and perfectly frames my large chest.

With one hand wrapped around my baby girl, I use my other one to apply a fresh coat of eyeliner and mascara. I have to juggle Paisley carefully because she keeps trying to grab for my makeup.

When I'm finally done with my face, I give myself a nod of approval in the bathroom mirror. "It's time to go meet your husband."

I settle in one of the cold metal chairs to watch the passengers come and go. But the entire time, I'm scanning the crowd and looking for one detail in particular. A man carrying a bouquet of violets.

There's one cowboy that catches my eye. He's tall, bearded, and big with the kind of confidence that shouts he knows what he wants and isn't afraid to go after it.

He's wearing tight Wranglers and a brown coat that's open and layered over a white, button down. His matching Stetson and boots make it obvious he's a local. I try to get a glimpse at his eyes but he's wearing dark aviator sunglasses. He moves gracefully and fluidly through the terminal, scanning for someone.

Even before I spot the violets he's carrying, I know he's my cowboy. I'm looking at my future husband and damn, the man is fine. With no pictures being exchanged through the mail-order bride service, I figured I'd get paired with someone that was old and crusty. This cowboy is definitely not those things.

I stand to greet the man who's already approaching me. He's like a magnet pulling me in, and I feel the attraction all the way to my toes. I've never felt this way and I don't know how to explain it.

When Paisley shivers in my arms, I tighten my hold on her. I remind myself that this cowboy will have to accept both of us for this marriage to work. I won't be like my mother and choose a man over my baby girl. No, we're a package deal and this is the moment of truth.

The cowboy reaches for his sunglasses and pulls them from his face. He's a good ten years older than me with laugh lines around the corners of his eyes. Now that I can see that gray-blue gaze, I relax a little.

There's something about his eyes. They're filled

with kindness and compassion. A reaction I didn't expect, and it throws me off-balance. I expected anger or frustration. Maybe even betrayal.

He tucks the sunglasses in his shirt pocket at the exact moment that Paisley lunges for him. She's never done that with anyone else, never reached out first.

To my surprise, the cowboy reaches for her and for a reason, I can't explain I let him hold her. He smiles down at her and asks in a Southern drawl that's as smooth as melted chocolate, "What's your name, pretty girl?"

"Her name is Paisley Jolene." My own voice comes out rough and scratchy. I've always figured my daughter would grow up like me, never having a real dad. But standing there with this big stranger cuddling my girl, I can't help but hope that I've been wrong.

"Well, hello there, Miss Paisley," he croons as he shrugs out of his coat while managing not to drop the flowers. He covers her with it and she snuggles into his chest. "What's your pretty mama's name?"

2

LOGAN

It's a simple mission: find and retrieve my bride. I step out of the truck at the Courage County Bus Station and carefully avoid a patch of ice on the ground. The snow from the storm earlier this week has melted and refrozen, leaving an icy wonderland beneath my feet.

I'm halfway into the terminal when I realize I left the flowers in my truck. The mail-order bride matchmaking service sent me flowers that I'm supposed to take. They're meant to symbolize something. I don't remember what though because when Laney, the matchmaker, was talking I was on video call in my greenhouse. Guess I should have paid her a little more attention.

My phone rings while I'm still outside. I take the time to answer the call from Sheriff Luke. "You got my Gator from Sticky yet?"

A Gator is a type of utility vehicle we use around the ranch. It makes it easy to get from place to place, haul supplies, and move equipment. Only mine disappeared last week. I already got a hunch who took it. Old Man Teller's teenage boy ain't called Sticky for nothing. He's had sticky fingers since he was five years old.

"Naw, just calling to let you know that I got your report and I'm gonna look into it," he answers. "And to wish you well on your wedding day. You and your bride need anything, you just holler."

I thank him for the well wishes, reminded of why I like living in a small town. Yeah, there are moments it's annoying to have everyone knowing your business. But there's also a small comfort in realizing people around you have your back.

When I have the flowers, I'm stalking through the station. I don't bother to remove my glasses. I don't want to stop and talk to any of the locals right now. I'm too amped up to make small talk about the weather or the Valentine's day dance happening in a couple of weeks. No, there's only one thing I'm here for right now. My wife.

I recognize most of the crowd, buzzing around the busy terminal. There are a few unfamiliar faces, tourists that come here looking to spend their winter vacation in a sweet, small town.

One woman grabs my attention. It's the too-tight, skimpy red tank and the blue jean skirt that lets me see miles of creamy thigh. The moment I register she's not dressed for the weather, I stomp toward her. The profile said my woman was coming from Miami. She's definitely not prepared for a Courage County winter.

But her deliciously long legs aren't the only thing that's caught my eye, she's holding a baby on her hip. A little thing that like her sweet mama isn't dressed for the conditions. She's got no shoes, only a pink onesie and a little headband with a sad-looking flower on it.

I glance at her mama's face and see the trepidation written there. I can practically read those honey brown eyes. She's expecting me to send her and her baby away.

For a split second, I'm thirteen again and wishing that someone would want me anyway. That split second is all it takes for me to decide I'm keeping them. Doesn't matter that she lied. I can find some way to make it work.

I pull my sunglasses from my face and clip them onto my shirt. Up close to her, I realize there's more than just despair and steely acceptance in her gaze. There's something else too. Fear, real and primal. This is about more than rejection. She's afraid of something or someone. The thought fills me with white, hot rage. No one will ever hurt her or her baby. I will guard them both with my life.

The little one lunges for me like she's been waiting all her life to meet me. Hours spent in the neonatal unit come rushing back to me and I reach for her instinctively. I can't help crooning down at her. She's about five pounds underweight for her size and I make a mental note to make sure her mama has more than enough formula on hand. "What's your name, pretty girl?"

"Her name is Paisley Jolene." Her mama has the prettiest voice I've ever heard. It's bluesy and soulful, reminding me of Etta James. I can't help but wonder what she sounds like when she sings. She doesn't look like the type that's had a lot of reason to sing in her life. No, she has the kind of haunted look that only another survivor recognizes.

"Well, hello there, Miss Paisley," I say as I peel off my jacket. I can't stand the thought that this precious little bundle is cold. "What's your pretty mama's name?"

Paisley snuggles deep into my chest, no doubt eager to get closer to the warmth. She's breaking my heart. Her and her young mama who can't be older than two decades. I don't know where the hell the man who's supposed to be looking after them is but I don't understand him. You look after your woman and your kids where I come from.

"Audrey," the woman finally says.

"Well, Audrey," I drawl the name out slow, liking the way it tastes in my mouth. "You ready to get hitched?"

Audrey

I CAN'T BELIEVE MY EARS WHEN HE ASKS IF I'M READY to get married. I'd waited for the past two days, expecting instant rejection. Instead, he's accepting us. Both of us. Just like that.

It feels too good to be true and I plant my feet. Experience with men has taught me that some conversations are better had in a public place with a lot of witnesses around. "What's the catch?"

He frowns. "What catch? We both agreed to this marriage."

"So you don't have a problem with Paisley?"

He glances down at my baby daughter that has not only curled up against his chest but is now quietly sleeping. *I'd like to sleep in his arms too.* I push the thought away immediately. Thinking I'd have someone come in and rescue me is what normally gets me into bad situations to start with.

"Who could have a problem with this little angel?"

"Why do you need to get married?" I bark out the words. Yeah, I'm a little bit on edge and maybe I could soften my delivery. But there's too much wrong here. He's too good-looking and too young and too instantly accepting.

Something in his stance softens. Instead of going on the defensive, he's relaxing around me. I don't understand this man at all. "Legal reasons and I gotta be honest with ya, it don't look like you and your girl here have a whole lot of other options."

He studies me for a long moment. Even though I'm used to men staring at me with lust, this is different. It's like he's trying to figure me out and I hate that more. Finally, he says, "If you want to leave right now, I'll get you a ticket home. Fully paid. No questions asked."

I nearly wilt beneath the weight of his words. I have no home. The closest thing I had was that crappy apartment. The crappy apartment that Calvin shoved his way into. An announcement comes on the speaker that the next bus is departing in thirty minutes.

My cowboy raises an eyebrow. "What will it be?"

I take the flowers from him, accepting the inevitable. "What if this doesn't work out?"

"It will," he answers with a confidence that makes me want to believe him. But I've been burned enough to know better than to trust in another hollow promise. "Now, come on. We have a stop to make before we do this."

The stop turns out to be at a clothing store. I guess my groom-to-be caught on to the fact that I have no luggage other than the baby car seat. The canvas tote I'm using as a diaper bag is way too light.

"We lost everything in a fire the night before we got on the bus," I lied to him.

He nodded, but I could tell from the slant of his mouth that he knew I was lying. Still, he didn't push for answers or ask questions. Instead, he shared a few facts about Courage County.

Now, we're standing in the middle of a department store in Asheville. It's obvious from the plush carpeting and the sales associate wearing pearls that I don't fit in here. I mind as well be walking in here naked for the way her judgmental gaze is narrowed in on me.

I keep my head held high and my shoulders pulled back. If there's one thing my time on the streets taught me, it's that weakness can be sensed.

Logan puts a hand on my back as the woman hurries over to us. He gives her a smile that probably gets him exactly what he wants in his hometown. "My wife lost her luggage while traveling and we need to quickly pick up a few basics."

"Of course," the smile she gives him makes something churn in my stomach. I don't like the way she's looking at him.

After an hour, I have things to get me through. Logan encouraged me several times to get whatever I wanted. But I felt funny about the idea of doing that. Every time I picked up a pair of jeans, I looked at the price tag and counted up how many hours I'd have to spend stripping to pay for it. The answer for most of them was too many.

It wasn't until I reached the clearance racks that I relaxed a little. The prices were still far more than what I'd spend on myself at the thrift store but at least, they weren't over the top.

My favorite thing though that we bought today was a coat for Paisley. It's a soft, pink one with little ears on the hood that make her look just like a cute, teddy bear. Not that she likes wearing the hood. She fusses each time I try to put it on her head.

Still, it makes me happy to see her in it. It makes me even happier to know she's warm now. I didn't realize how heavily that was weighing on me until she was all wrapped up.

Logan taps his fingers against his knee as he drives us to Courage County for our upcoming nuptials. "I'll only ask you once and never bring it up again. But where about is Paisley's father?"

I sigh, wishing I knew the answer to that one. "I have no idea. He was a one-night stand I met at a bar. I've been back since then, but I think he was passing through the city."

"So he doesn't even know she exists? Damn, that'd kill me to miss out on her life." He sounds so sad, so full of despair.

Not for the first time I wish I'd gotten more information about the stranger. "Like I said, I've been back to the bar. I posted a couple of times online, looking for him. You know those missed connections? If he's seen the post, he's never gotten back to me."

We never discussed what he did for a living, where he was from, or anything that would give me a clue where to start looking. Outside of putting her DNA in one of those databases when she's older, I don't know how to connect with him.

Logan lets the conversation drop after that. He seems lost in thought and I don't really want to talk about this anymore. It makes me sad for Paisley that she doesn't have a dad in her life.

Finally, Logan pulls his truck into the parking lot of a wedding chapel in the heart of the town. The tiny white building is glowing with light from the inside in the early evening and above the door is a simple inscription, "All are welcome here".

It's warm inside and smells of orange and lavender. A sense of peace washes over me as I stand in the foyer. The minister, who's wearing blue overalls and a checked shirt, rushes from a back office to greet Logan. He claps him on the back then looks at Paisley with affection. "What a precious little girl. We're so glad to have you both joining us today."

Not for the first time, I wonder if I've found somewhere to belong. A tiny town that holds open its arms to a single mom and her baby. Would they still be so accepting if they knew what I've done? Would Logan?

I risk a glance at the man that's about to be my husband. He's chatting with the minister about crops or something. I'm not paying too much attention. Instead, I excuse myself to a backroom with Paisley.

After a diaper change and her last bottle, she's feeling happy again. "Our lives are looking up, aren't they?"

She grins at me as if agreeing and puts her chubby fist in her mouth. Since she's started teething, she loves to chew on her hand.

I keep my voice pitched low as I wipe some of the drool from her chin with a bib. This man thought of everything she might need. "And that feels pretty wonderful right now. But let's not get too attached, OK?"

Her face crumples as if my words are sinking in and making her feel just as sad and heavy as I do. It'd be nice to belong somewhere. To have people looking out for us and taking care of us. But I think I ruined that after Calvin. No one is going to believe me or defend me.

I rock her against my chest and whisper that her mom is here and she's never leaving. We're all we've ever had and no matter how much I like this handsome cowboy, I don't imagine we'll be staying forever.

He said he had to get married for legal reasons. That means there's probably an end date in his mind. I just have to figure out how to stand on my own two feet before then.

3
AUDREY

WHEN I STEP OUT OF THE BACKROOM, I PAUSE TO smooth down my long-sleeved green dress that I purchased at the department store. I love the full skirt and wraparound design with the bow on the side that draws the eye to my curvy hips. The sweetheart neckline is soft and feminine without being too low cut. For the first time in a long time, I feel beautiful.

Logan stands from where he was sitting in one of the tiny pews with another man. There are only three pews on each side of the small chapel. I don't imagine it's big enough to hold more than ten or so guests at a time. But somehow, I love it more for that. I love that Logan chose something small, intimate, and quiet for our vows.

He scans me in the outfit, appreciation obvious in his gaze. "You look beautiful, Audrey."

Paisley grunts from her place in my arms. She's been grumpy ever since I told her not to get attached to Logan.

He leans close to her, giving her a big grin. "So do you, Miss Paisley."

The man that was in the chapel pew rises to his feet and pauses to adjust the top button on his blue button down.

"This is my brother, Ethan. Ethan, this is Audrey, my future wife." He says the last three words with emphasis, giving his brother a pointed glare.

I don't know what's happened between them but I'm guessing that Ethan doesn't like me. I nod to him. I don't need him to like me. I just need him to not look into my background.

The look Ethan gives me tells me that he's not happy, but he doesn't say anything to me. Instead, he just turns to the reverend. "Are we about to get this show on the road?"

I meant to remember the details of the wedding, but everything passes by in a blur of nervousness and repeating vows.

Ethan holds Paisley during the ceremony. But he's different around her than Logan is. He's clearly not sure what to do with a baby while Logan took right to her. It's strange because Logan's profile said he'd never had children. Yet he always seems to know what to do with Paisley.

When it's over, Logan brushes the briefest of kisses against my lips. I barely feel it and sign my name to a certificate in a daze. Just like that, I'm a married woman. The moment feels surreal. I never imagined I'd be married at eighteen with a baby and on the run. Except my husband doesn't know that last part. He never can.

———

Logan

"You're being an idiot," Ethan hissed at me as he watched Audrey and Paisley slip into the backroom of the chapel to get ready. "She's using that baby and that terrified help-me expression to ensnare you."

If it were anybody else who said it, I would have punched them on the spot. But not Ethan. Ethan found out last year in front of the whole town that his wife was cheating on him and the baby she was carrying wasn't his. That shit has got to leave a mark. It's the only thing that's keeping me in check right now.

"She needs me," I answer, feeling anger rise up in me.

"She's playing you. I'd bet anything she's hiding something," he insists.

I don't doubt for a moment that Audrey is hiding something from me. Probably a lot of somethings if we're being honest. But I also know that you can't fake the level of fear I saw in her eyes. Whatever the threat is, it's very real.

"You're going to be my best man or not?" I demand of my brother with a low warning growl in my tone. He knows to drop it.

Ethan studies me for a long moment before finally holding up his hands in surrender. "I don't want to see you get hurt."

Out of all my foster brothers, I'm closest to Ethan. He's the one that's been there for me count-less times and I was the one he leaned on after the blow up with his wife. "This will be a good thing."

Now I'm back in my truck with Audrey and Pais-ley. The wedding went well and it's over now. I wish I'd had a way to prepare a great big reception for my two girls, something to really welcome them into the Scott family.

Audrey has been quiet ever since the wedding and a part of me wonders if she regrets it already.

"I figure I'll show you the house then we can go into town for supplies," I explain.

She yawns in the fading light and I remember that she's been on a bus for the past two days. They both have to be exhausted.

I quickly correct myself, "I'll show you the house then go into town for supplies. Just make me a list of what I can get for you both."

I already know she has to need formula and diapers. That little thing she called a diaper bag didn't weight practically anything. There's no chance she had more than a bottle or two in there.

We lost everything in a fire the night before we got on the bus.

That was definitely bullshit, but I didn't call her on it. I figure I'll spend some time earning her trust before I try to delve into her past.

"Wow, this is your place?" She asks when I pull in front of the one-story ranch home. I try to look at it through her eyes. It's a plain little house that could definitely use a woman's touch. Maybe I should have done something to the front of it before I went and got her. Not that I suppose it matters too much. The slushy snow would have hidden my hard work anyway.

"This is *our* place," I correct her gently. I want her to know she has a home now. She has that lost look in her eyes that I recognize from being a foster kid. It makes my heart hurt to see it on her face.

"Our place," she repeats the phrase softly as she stares up at the house. There's something in those honey brown eyes. I want to ask her a million questions and learn her every secret. But out of all people, I understand that trust must be earned. It can't be demanded or coerced.

"Let me show you and Miss Paisley around," I say as I leave the truck. I grab the bags from our earlier shopping trip. It was almost painful to watch her shop. It's clear she's used to foraging for what meager handouts that life will give her but that's over.

Now, she has someone that will provide for her and her child. I'll give her everything that her heart could desire. I'll make her my queen and spoil her night and day. Paisley will be our princess and she'll never know anything but love and kindness. Whether Audrey realizes it or not, this is a new day in their lives.

"My brothers and I all live on the ranch," I

explain to her as I lead her up the walk. "But we have separate residences spread out over the land. Grandpa let us throw dice for the parcels and that's how it was decided."

I may have been angry about Grandpa's plan to force me into this marriage, but the man has always tried to do right by the eight of us, despite the fact that none of the boys he helped raise were biologically his. It takes a strong man to love a generation of rag-tag kids that are scarred from a lifetime of abuse.

I show Audrey around the place, surprised by how much I hope she likes my home. It's far from fancy but something tells me that even this might be an upgrade from where she's come from. The idea makes me sick to my stomach. I don't want to think about the terrible situation that she and her child were probably in or what would have happened to them if I hadn't been the one to match with her.

"It's beautiful." She gives me a small smile when she's finished the grand tour of the open concept living room, kitchen, and dining room.

"I'll give you a tour of the rest of the place."

The bathroom and two spare bedrooms aren't much to look at. But the master bedroom is my favorite. It's also a place I've never taken a woman. I never wanted somebody in my home. But with Audrey, it's different. She and Paisley belong here. Who knew when I built this little cottage that one day I'd have a wife and child to share it with? If only Mrs. Scott could see me now. She'd love Audrey and her sweet baby.

"Whoa," Audrey says when we step into the master bedroom. The wall of glass windows that lets me look out and watch the rising sun is my favorite feature. It brightens up the whole place. But tonight with the sun already setting and painting the room in hues of purple and pink, it's even prettier than usual.

"I bet it's a sight to wake up to," she whispers.

I bet you're a sight to wake up to. I don't say the words even though I'm thinking them. But I can't stop myself from glancing toward my Alaskan King bed and wondering what she would look like in it with her golden-brown hair spilling across my pillow.

"It's something alright," I answer, my voice coming out deeper than normal.

Paisley makes a noise of delight and says something in her cute little baby talk that I can't make out.

"I think she likes it here," her pretty mama chuckles.

That's when I realize I don't have a crib or well, any of the furniture you need for a baby. Damn, there's a lot of things I need to get around to doing.

"Do you have any family to help you with her?" I ask. Yeah, I want to go slow and win her trust. But I'm also curious if she has anybody in her corner. Surely, there's got to be a concerned grandparent or someone who gives a damn about them.

The smile she gives me is tinged with sadness. She crosses her arms and says in a flat tone, "I've been on my own since I was fourteen. Complained to my mom about my stepfather putting his hands all over me and ended up getting tossed onto the streets. I got pregnant at seventeen, and it's been a hell of a ride, Logan."

I let out a slow whistle. I hate that she's spent the past four years alone. Still, her strength shines through everything she does. She's a warrior even if she doesn't see it. "I can only imagine."

Audrey yawns again, pausing to cover her mouth with her hand. That little gold band on her finger winks at me, a reminder of what we did today. We intertwined our lives forever and ever. I thought the idea would make me feel like panicking but strangely, it doesn't.

"What can I get you from the store?"

She shakes her head. "You've already done enough."

I fight a wave of annoyance. I get that she's not used to leaning on anyone and that's not likely to change in just a few hours. But I'm not asking because I'm being polite. I *want* to take care of them. It surprises me just how fierce and overwhelming the need is to provide for my girls. "At least, tell me the brand of formula she prefers."

She gives me that, and I manage to get a little bit more information before I press a kiss to her forehead. I want to do a hell of a lot more than that to the woman in my bedroom. But I settle for the softest brush of my lips against her skin. Pretty soon I'll kiss her in other ways, ways she'll be begging me for.

"Wait," she calls right before I leave the house.

I pause on my way out the door, watching as she shifts her weight from foot to foot. I like how it makes the full skirt of the dress swish. Damn, I want my head to be under that skirt, tasting her and bringing her body pleasure.

She licks her lips then looking almost pained she says, "Thank you."

I can tell from her expression they're not words she's used to saying, so I just nod and give her a small smile. "Things are going to be better now."

4
LOGAN

THE GROCERY TRIP TAKES FOREVER. FOR EVERY TYPE of baby product, there are about three hundred different options. It's enough to make any new parent feel overwhelmed.

Fortunately, Miss Emma May, who owns the largest grocery store in Courage County, takes pity on me. The woman has raised five of her own kids and taken in countless others over the years.

Within a few minutes, she has me sorted. I swipe my credit card and I'm almost home when I realize I still don't have a crib. Emma's place isn't big enough to stock furniture.

Jake owns Taylor Furnishings, but he specializes in custom-built stuff. Every now and again, he has something readymade for sale that a client decided not to finish purchasing. But it's pretty rare which means the odds of him having a crib aren't good.

That's when I remember the old stuff. There was a ton of things from our foster parents that Ranger put in storage. We're the last generation on the farm and it's not like we've all been popping out babies.

The old workshop has a thick padlock around it, so I have to drive to Ranger's place before I can even open it.

He grunts when he opens the front door. I almost feel bad for interrupting him today. He said something about taking time off to spend with his new wife. I met Tia the other day, and she's good for my brother. He smiles more in the past few days than he has in years. "Do you not understand the concept of vacation time?"

"You're the one who put the family things in storage. Where is the key?" I demand. I know Ranger is just keeping up with shit. He doesn't actually want to prevent any of us from having access.

"I have it around here somewhere." He gestures for me to follow him into his house as he wheels around. He's been in a motorized scooter as long as I've known him. I hated how he got treated in high school and got suspended more than once for kicking ass on his behalf. Watching him get bullied every day for four years wasn't something I could just stand by and do.

While Ranger goes on the search, I wait in the living room with Tia. She's a shy little thing, and after everything I've seen happen with her, I know she came from a bad situation. Not unlike my Audrey.

"How did the wedding go?" She asks.

"Great," I mutter, not sure how to describe the whole thing. I mean, it went off without a problem other than Ethan opening his big mouth. At least, he had the decency not to say anything to Audrey. That definitely would have earned him a black eye.

Range wheels into the room with the key in hand. "What do you need from storage so urgently?"

"A crib."

He stops his chair. "Things don't happen that fast."

"I need a crib. Figure the one that's been passed down will do just fine. My woman showed up with a baby on her hip," I explain, cramming my Stetson back on my head. I just want to get my girls comfortable.

"And you married her anyway?" Tia asks. There's no judgment in her tone, only curiosity.

But it's the look on my older brother's face that

tells me he's not happy. Like Ethan, he's worried that I did something stupid. Hell, maybe I did. But I wasn't about to leave Audrey or Paisley there at the bus station. They need a defender and I'll be proud to step into that role. "You should have seen them, Range. Two sets of scared little eyes."

"I hope you know what you're getting yourself into." It's what Ranger said right before I smashed up Bryce's car for giving him a swirly in the high school bathroom. I'm the type of cowboy that defends those around me. It's how I'm built. I can't ignore someone in distress.

Tia glares at her new husband and I have to smother a laugh. They've only been married for three days and they're already falling into married couple patterns. I wonder if that'll happen to me and Audrey.

"We'll be here if you need anything," my new sister-in-law promises.

I tip my hat at her. Audrey might need a friend while she's adjusting to life on our ranch. Something tells me that Tia won't hesitate to make her feel welcome. "Thanks for that. Might take you up on it."

As I leave, I can't help the spring in my step. I didn't expect that Grandpa knew what he was doing with this whole plan of his. After all, I've never believed that soulmates exist. But after today, there's a small part of me that wants to.

Audrey

ONCE LOGAN IS GONE, THE FULL WEIGHT OF WHAT I've done strikes me. I've married a complete stranger. A man I don't know is now my husband. I can't even tell you his favorite color or what type of cuisine he prefers. That information was probably on his profile, but I didn't pay too much attention at the time. I just agreed to the first man who accepted me.

The house suddenly feels too tiny and it's too hard to breathe in here. While we were coming in, I saw a greenhouse in Logan's yard. I figure the cold air will do me and Paisley some good and step into the backyard.

A small brick path leads to the greenhouse that's made entirely of glass. It's about the size of a barn and the moment I step inside, I'm greeted by the scent of onions. He's growing all sorts of vegetables in here.

"Didn't take you for a man with a green thumb," I

say. Logan strikes me as someone that likes to jump in with both feet and worry about the consequences of what he's done later. That seems at odds with a man who is patient enough to garden during the winter season.

When I finally feel like I can breathe again, I head back into the house. It's warm and cozy, so different from anywhere else I've lived.

Since we're still alone, I treat myself and Paisley to a nice, warm bath. It feels luxurious after spending the past few weeks washing up in gas station restrooms and other public facilities.

"He likes you," I tell Paisley. It was obvious from the first moment he looked at her that he felt a connection with her. It eased something in my heart to see that, the way they both took to each other.

She splashes the water and giggles.

"Not sure how he feels about me," I admit. I think about how his gaze kept straying to the bed when we were in his room. Lust and like are two very different things. Lust is something a lot of men have looked at me with. But to be liked would be some-thing new and intoxicating. I shake my head. "Your mom is being silly."

When Logan comes home, I'll make sure to seduce him. I won't give him a reason to kick us out.

After all, he's good to Paisley and as for husbands, I could have done worse. He's considerate, kind, and seems to accept my daughter. There's a lot to be thankful for.

My skin has wrinkled, and I've refilled the bathtub with warm water twice before I finally force myself from it. Paisley falls asleep easily dressed in her little pajamas on the king-size bed. I surround her with giant pillows and watch her. She seems at peace here.

Since I forgot to buy pajamas for myself, I slip into one of his shirts. I like the way it smells like him, a mixture of earth and leather. *A man of the land*, I think to myself as I crawl into bed beside Paisley and wait for my cowboy husband to come home.

It's morning when I open my eyes again and for a moment, I can't remember why I'm not in my car. Then I remember the events of the past two days, boarding the bus and meeting Logan. I glance down at the ring on my finger. It's a simple gold band, and I tell myself it doesn't mean anything.

Paisley is still in bed beside me, but Logan isn't here. I wonder if he came home as I sit up. Then I spot the crib in the corner of the room.

It's clearly a vintage one made of light oak with thin spindles. On the headboard, a smiling teddy bear has been painted. Over the years some of the paint has faded, but it's still beautiful.

I run my hands along the solid piece of furniture. I imagine generations of little cowboys have slept in this. Now Paisley will too. The idea makes me smile.

Since she's still sleeping, I take a minute in the bathroom before I decide to find myself some breakfast. I stop when I step into the living room.

Logan is asleep on the tiny couch, his six-foot frame dwarfing the furniture. His legs hang off one end, and his head is twisted at an angle that has to be painful on his neck. He's snoring softly, his face peaceful and relaxed.

On his chest is a still-open book about making your home safe for your infant. That's when I realize the glass coffee table that was in front of the couch is gone.

"You're taking this so seriously," I murmur as I move to the kitchen. There are covers on all the sockets. I'm pretty sure they weren't there yesterday, and the cabinets have safety latches on them now. I should tell him that she's not even crawling yet.

The table is loaded with baby formula, diapers, bottles, wipes, and other essentials. There's easily a three-month supply of everything. I shake my head at the man. "You don't do anything halfway."

I make breakfast for both of us. I'm not a great cook, but I can make cheesy scrambled eggs and bacon. That and a pot of coffee seem like a good way to start the day.

Logan grunts when he finally comes into the kitchen. His hair is poking out in different directions and he absently massages his neck while he pours himself a cup of coffee. I don't know how he's making bedhead look sexy.

"Did you sleep OK?" I ask to distract myself.

He starts to nod then grimaces. "Great. How about you two?"

I tell him that I did then reach on tiptoes for the plates on the top shelf of the cabinet. When I turn back to him, there's heat in his gaze. I realize too late that his t-shirt must have come up higher on my hips. I probably gave him a great view of my ass, but judging from that look, the man doesn't mind.

It's a good thing he's looking at me that way. It'll be easier to seduce him.

Paisley stirs in the other room, making a soft cooing noise. I hurry from the kitchen to her. When I return, Logan is reading the instructions for a can of formula. He's studying it so seriously that I can't help but smile. "Here, let me show you."

The three of us settle for breakfast and he says, "I

have chores around the farm this morning. But I couldn't get everything Paisley needed last night. So, let's go into the city this afternoon and get it."

"How could you have not gotten everything she needed?" I'm sure he means well, but he's clearly going overboard. "Logan, I like what you're trying to do but she's one tiny baby. Hell, we're used to living out of my car."

He swallows a bite of bacon and pins me with that gray-blue gaze I've already come to like so much. "And how did that come to be?"

Another man thought he could own me.

"It just did," I say as I set the bottle on the table and adjust Paisley to burp her. She starts wailing like I knew she would.

But Logan doesn't drop the subject. As soon as she's guzzling more formula, he focuses on me. "You don't have to be scared anymore. Whatever it is that you were running from, I'll protect you now."

I'd love to believe him. I'd love to have someone in my corner to help me fight my battles, but I learned a long time ago that life doesn't work that way. Instead, I force a bright smile I don't feel. "Where in the city did you want to go?"

5

AUDREY

WHILE LOGAN IS GONE, I START UP HIS LAPTOP. HE
told me to use anything I wanted in the house and
promised to be back in a few hours. He even kissed
me on the forehead again. Paisley too.

Since he gave me blanket permission to whatever
I want, I open up the history in his browser. The
only thing in it are searches for gardening sites,
which isn't surprising given the greenhouse out
back.

A new chat window opens on the screen,
revealing a conversation between him and Ethan.
Actually, it appears to be a group chat with him and
I'm guessing his brothers. They're going back and
forth, making bets on which teams will make it to

the Superbowl. I smile as I read through their banter. Apparently, my husband is a diehard Packers fan. They're all mocking him for it, and he's taking it good-naturedly.

I chuckle and eventually minimize the chat window, so I can start searching the surrounding areas of Courage County. I make a list of all the area bars, specifically noting the ones that have dancers.

I was an up-and-comer in the stripping scene in Miami. I was making more money than ever before, and my life was finally coming together. If it hadn't been for Calvin, a patron who became obsessed with me, I wouldn't have moved to North Carolina to marry a sexy cowboy.

A sexy cowboy with a deep voice and scratchy beard.

I wonder what it would be like to run my fingers through it and dismiss the thought just as Paisley lets out a squeal of delight. She's on a playmat in the floor beside me, staring up at the jungle-themed toys.

She bats them and giggles when the colorful toucan swings just out of her reach. This is one of three different mats Logan brought home last night. I suspect I'll need to spend a lot of time trying to keep him from spoiling her. Except that we won't be here forever.

Logan might be enamored with us now, but he admitted that he needed a wife for legal reasons. I'm sure that will change eventually, and I want to be prepared to care for Paisley. I want to give her a good life.

"Things are turning around for us," I promise my little girl. It's a promise that I plan to keep, no matter what it takes.

Logan

"SHE REALLY DOESN'T NEED A PINK CHANDELIER FOR her nursery," Audrey insists as we're standing in the middle of the home goods store here in Asheville. She's pinching the bridge of her nose and looking frustrated with me again.

I pull my eyes from the package that features those pink drop things that look like jewels. She's already my little princess and I want to spoil her with everything good in this world.

Paisley pats my beard as if she's agreeing with her mama on this one. They've already talked me out of getting a canopy to put above the crib. Audrey was worried about the fabric posing a suffocation risk.

Audrey's gaze softens when she looks at me. I like it when she does that, drops just a little of her armor. She gestures toward the cart that's nearly overflowing. "Most little girls never get half this stuff, and they turn out just fine."

"It's not about her being just fine. She deserves more than that," I argue. It's hard to explain to her what it's like to know you came into the world and were immediately tossed into a dumpster, to know that no one celebrated you or even cared that you were here. I want it to be different for Paisley. I want her to understand that I'm always going to be her champion, the one that celebrates her and reminds her how special she is.

Audrey steps forward and puts a hand over my heart. "She has you in her corner right now."

My heart speeds up under her gentle touch. I nod, not trusting my voice.

"That's more than many girls have. Now, come on. Let's get her home before the temperatures drop outside." She nods to the glass doors to the store. In the fading light, I can see that more snow has started to fall.

I grumble but follow her to the checkout desk. I

pass her the squirming little girl so I can pull my credit card from my wallet. All those years of living frugally because I didn't need the latest truck or a new fishing boat were definitely worth it now that I have my girls to dote on. I'll spend every last cent to make them happy.

"Lord love a duck! I thought that was you, Logan Scott!" Lorraine Edwards declares. She is the secretary at Courage County High School.

The woman was so old when I was in high school that the rumor was the school was built around her. You'd think that given she's nearly ninety she would have slowed down. But she's got more energy and spunk than most women half her age. Given how often I was called to the principal's office for causing trouble, I had a lot of time to get to know her. We sort of became friends.

I turn to the pint-sized woman and she instantly reaches to engulf me in a hug. She reminds me of Mrs. Scott and a wave of grief surprises me. I close my eyes against the unexpected visitor.

Grief is a strange thing. You think you've seen him for the last time then he shows up when you're standing in the middle of the home goods store and wishing you could introduce your wife and baby girl to the only woman who was like a mama to you. But since I can't do that, I clear my throat and step back. "It's good to see you, Mrs. Eddie. Let me introduce you to my wife, Audrey, and my daughter, Paisley Jolene."

Just like that I realize that Paisley is my daughter. I don't even know when I claimed her. I just know that she and her pretty mama are mine now.

"Oh, welcome to the family, dear!" She engulfs Audrey in an equally big hug, careful not to squish Paisley between them. She steps back to admire my little daughter and I feel a rush of pride, something primal in my chest that knows these two belong with me.

She chats with us for a few minutes before she leaves to go find her husband in another part of the store.

"They seem nice," Audrey remarks once we're settled in my truck and on the way back home. Damn, I love the sound of that. Home. I have a home now, a family to share it with. The knowledge warms something in my chest.

I glance in the backseat, checking on Paisley. The little girl is staring out the window at the falling snow in wide-eyed wonder. I love the way everything is still new and fascinating to her. "People 'round here are like that."

Audrey follows my gaze. "How many nieces and nephews do you have?"

"None." I already know where she's going with this.

"It seems you've taken to Paisley so naturally, but your profile said you didn't have kids of your own." Confusion is coloring her tone.

I war with what to tell her about my past. I should probably be honest, but I don't see a point in telling her my sad story. "I've been around babies here and there."

"Does Courage County have a lot of single moms in desperate need of help with their babies?"

I didn't imagine the jealous note in her voice, and it makes me smile. I don't know why I feel good knowing that she's possessive. "Not exactly."

We continue the trip in silence, and I don't know what to say or how to bring it up. With the dark sky and the snow blowing around us, I figure I can at least try to tell her something. "The hospital in Asheville has a neonatal unit for sick and premature babies, and it has a cuddle program."

"So you go and cuddle the children?" She asks.

To get accepted into the program, I had to undergo specialized training, volunteer in another department, and pass a background check. Like every volunteer, I'm still carefully supervised.

My ranch hands know that twice a week I cut out early. They don't know what I do or where I go. Hell, I've never told Ethan. I don't even know why I'm telling her. "Yeah, some parents can't be there with their little ones. They might have work or family obligations. Maybe it's just too far for them to travel to be with their baby each day. That's where the volunteers come in. We cuddle the babies, sing with them, talk to them."

It hurts my heart to think that there are parents who can't be with their premature or sick child. I'd be wrecked if Paisley needed me and I couldn't be with her. I wouldn't be able to sleep, eat, or function.

Audrey is quiet for a long time then finally as I'm pulling the truck into our driveway, she asks, "How'd you get started cuddling?"

After I traced my own history back and learned I was abandoned in a dumpster, a lot of things made sense to me. Why I felt so different from other people, how I struggled to make connections, and form relationships. Those things that come naturally to kids who are held and loved and cuddled. I never had that, but I figured I could give it to some babies who needed it. Maybe give them a better life than I had.

"I read about it online," I lie, not willing to tell her more. If I do, she'll know I'm garbage and I don't want her looking at me that way. She looks at me like I'm her hero and that makes me feel like I could wrestle a bull with my bare hands. I'm not willing to lose that.

6

LOGAN

She sleeps a lot. The realization wouldn't bother me about Paisley. According to the book I'm reading, she needs an average of fourteen hours of sleep every day. But Audrey is a grown woman.

Paisley started fussing for dinner as we came in the door and I told Audrey to go feed her. While she was giving our daughter a bottle, I hauled our purchases in the house.

By the time I was done, they were both asleep in my bed. It warms me that they fall asleep so easily there. But it also worries me. When was the last time they both felt safe and warm? Why are there those dark circles under their eyes? Who gave them that look of fear? I don't have answers to these questions, but I know I will be their safe harbor. When the storms of life come, they can run to me and I'll be the one that shields and protects them.

Standing here, watching them sleep, I know without a doubt they're mine now. Mine to shelter and protect. Mine to provide for and champion. Mine to nurture and love.

Audrey startles awake, a look of absolute terror on her face for a half-second before she realizes where she is and who she's with.

"You're safe," I tell her, instinctively knowing that she needs the reassurance.

She turns her head to check on Paisley. Her features relax as soon as she sees that her little girl is sleeping peacefully next to her. I've already put pillows on the other side of the bed, so she won't roll off. The book said that she's old enough to start rolling herself over though I haven't asked Audrey about that one yet.

"She's fine. Let's get you some dinner," I tell her as I set up the video monitor. It was an impulse purchase I grabbed on our way out of the store and now I'm glad I did. This small device will give us both peace of mind as we get the nursery decorated.

After dinner, we clean out one of the spare bedrooms. Mainly, it's a process of moving boxes from one room to the next. The boxes are high school uniforms from my football days and gardening books that were passed down to me from Mrs. Scott.

Doing this reminds me that I have a whole life here while Audrey arrived with nothing but the clothes on her back. I plan to find a way to get her to trust me. I want to know the darkness that haunts her so I can protect her. Her and little Paisley.

But to do that, I need to form a connection. I need to give her a reason to open up to me. I try to recall her profile as I watch her bend over to pour the paint into the tray. She's wearing those tiny, short type things that women wear sometimes as underwear. They're stretched tight across her perfect heart-shaped ass, and I have to look away so I can remember what I was trying to think about. *Win her trust first. Protect her then bed her.*

Too bad my cock wants to do all of that backwards.

"On your profile, you said you were a dancer," I say when she straightens with the roller in her hand. Fuck me, she's not wearing a bra underneath that old thin t-shirt of mine and she has more than generous tits. Maybe double Ds or bigger. "What— what kind of dancing? Ballet, ballroom?"

She's got a dancer's figure alright. An image of us

tangoing together fills my mind and I have to fight a groan. I try to focus on the wall I'm supposed to be painting. The color is a bright, cheerful yellow that Audrey chose.

"The erotic kind." She turns to me, holding my stare as she says, "I know that in a small town like this, you probably think I should be embarrassed. But when you've done the things I've done just to have a place to sleep and food to eat, you lose your sense of shame. Life is really simple when your only goal is to survive to the next day."

I chuckle even though I'm not amused. She thinks we're so different. She doesn't realize we're cut from the same cloth. We're both survivors.

"Come here." I put my roller down and take two steps toward her. I hold out my hand and wrap her fingers around the base of my second finger. "Feel that? I cracked the knuckle punching one of the bigger boys at my sixth foster home. It never healed right."

Understanding flickers across her features as she lightly massages the area. If we weren't talking about this, I'd welcome her touch. Instead, I reach for the side of my shirt and pull it up, just far enough for her to catch a glimpse of the scars the extension cord left. "This was the boy's home when I was a teenager.

I still can't stand the sound of anything whistling through the air."

"Logan…"

I drop my shirt and put a hand under her chin, tilting her face up. I didn't show her this for pity. "I don't judge you for doing what it takes to make it through. I'm glad that you did. Morality and choices are luxuries for people like us. We do what we have to do, and we try not to let it haunt us."

She looks like she wants to say something and for a moment, I think I've gotten through to her. But then the video monitor lets the sound of Paisley's cries fill the room. Just like that, her defenses slip back into place. She's not going to tell me a damn thing.

I watch her leave the room and curse the timing. *How am I going to protect her when I don't know what threat is coming?*

Audrey

I SING SOFTLY TO PAISLEY. THE ENTIRE TIME I'M aware the video monitor is on and there's so much I want to tell Logan. I thought he was this cowboy who'd had an easy, perfect life growing up in a small town.

But he was a foster kid and he's seen some pretty intense things if those scars are anything to go by. It makes me cringe to think of anyone hurting my cowboy husband. He's got the biggest heart of any man I've ever known. *He's still a man.*

The pull low in my belly is back at the thought. I saw the way he kept checking me out while we were painting. He tried to hide it, but the unmistakable look of male appreciation was in his gaze. I'd be lying if I said I didn't bend over for longer after that, didn't let my t-shirt dip down a little further. He thought I didn't see the way he adjusted his pants or the way he hissed out a breath when I let my chest graze against his arm.

When Paisley has finally quieted, I put her in the crib. Logan insisted on buying a new mattress for it today. He'd read something about suffocation risks with old baby mattresses. The man is quickly becoming an encyclopedia on fatherhood. If I were planning to stick around, I'd love to watch him raise Paisley. Something tells me he'd be an amazing dad.

Logan has just finished putting the last of the paint on the walls when I step into the room. The windows are open, letting in the fresh scent of cool winter air. It feels good against my overheated skin.

"I guess all there is to do is wait now," I say, eyeing him. Surely, he'll make a move now. He has to sense the tension between us, and he'll act on it.

He gives me a grin and produces a deck of cards. "I thought I could teach you to play poker while we wait."

I work to keep my expression casual, dropping my gaze to my feet. "I don't know. I'm not very good at cards."

"It's fun. We'll play strip poker," he says.

I look up at him through lowered lashes even as excitement builds in me. He clearly wants to see me naked or he wouldn't have suggested this game. "You'll go easy on me because I'm a newbie?"

"Sure," he answers with full confidence as he settles on the hardwood floor. He's spread out a blanket across from himself and he pats it. "Have a seat. We'll focus on learning the basics."

Logan gives me a rundown of the various poker hands. I slow him down twice and ask questions. He's patient with me, using cards from the deck to illustrate his point. Then he deals the first hand.

"So, is this good?" I ask when I show him my full house.

"Good but not as nice as four of a kind," he answers, revealing his cards.

I remove my sock then the next one. By the third hand, I've removed my necklace. It's one I got out of a gumball machine years ago with a dragon pendant. I thought it was both pretty and fierce, so I've kept it with me over the years.

"Can I deal now?" I ask on the fourth hand. It's not lost on me that the room is very warm despite the windows that are letting the air circulate to dry the paint. He must have turned the heat on high in the house to get it this warm. I have to hand it to my husband for thinking through everything. "This is not your first rodeo, is it, cowboy?"

He frowns. "Meaning?"

"It's not the first time you've tried to get a woman naked," I say as I deal. He's busy focusing on my face, not what my hands are doing. This is going to be even easier than I thought.

A mixture of emotions flicker across his face. Grief. Loss. Frustration. "I started sleeping around in high school and got a reputation. I spent most of my adult life living up to it until the last couple of years."

I glance at my hand of cards even though I already know what's under here. One pair. "But there's more to it than that."

He hesitates, searching for the words. He tosses two cards aside and waits for two fresh ones before he rearranges his hand again. "Because of…the boys' home and other things, I don't get along well with men that are older than me."

I feel a wave of sadness at his words. I know what it's like to grow up thinking that the men around you can't be trusted. Instead of having fun and learning about the world around you like the other kids, you're watching your back. You can't spend time developing friendships or caring about people. You're too busy surviving.

"When I came here, Mrs. Scott took me under her wing. She loved gardening and taught me everything I know. After she died, I was just…lost for a long time. I think, girls were a good distraction." He reveals a straight of two through six.

I remove my ponytail holder.

He narrows his eyes even as his face lights up. He likes my hair down. I noticed it earlier when we were shopping for the nursery supplies. "I'm not sure that counts as clothing."

I shrug, knowing that it will make his big shirt fall off my shoulder. His eyes track the movement as I deal the next hand. "Is she why you have the greenhouse in the backyard?"

The loss is back on his face. "When the cancer treatments left her weak, I'd wheel her out to her greenhouse. She had this big, beautiful glass one. I'd take her out there and she'd tell me what to do step-by-step. I'd give anything for one more afternoon of her clucking over her plants and fussing at me to be careful with them."

"She sounds wonderful," I tell him, feeling a pang of wistfulness. I wish I'd been close to my mom. Most of our bonding moments centered around me pulling her out of a puddle of her own puke and forcing her into the shower.

"She would have liked you and little Paisley." He frowns when he realizes he lost the hand. But still, he removes his left boot without protest. He loses three more hands in a row, and I watch his frustration mount.

"Beginner's luck," he mutters.

"Didn't take you for a sore loser," I tease back. Still, I purposely lose the next hand and remove my bracelet.

He loses again and peels off his white t-shirt. I figured the man would be built from all those hours on the farm, but I wasn't prepared for the sight that would greet me. His pecs have a light dusting of dark hair and his rippling six-pack is perfectly defined.

Underneath his belly button is a strip of hair that leads to the top of his pants. I can't help licking my lips.

"I saw that!" He insists.

I realize too late that he caught me dealing from the bottom of the deck. "Saw what?"

In one smooth motion, he tackles me and his big body lands over mine. "You're cheating."

7

AUDREY

"You're cheating," Logan says as he pins me to the hardwood floor. His eyes are filled with amusement despite the way that he's gathered up my wrists and is holding them above my head.

"I'm not cheating. I'm playing to my strengths." I take a deep breath, feeling the way my nipples tighten to sharp points. My thin t-shirt is the only barrier between our chests. I see it register on his face too. The moment he realizes that he's lying on top of me.

He drops his head and seals his lips to mine. His taste is warm and spicy, like the cinnamon candies he's always sucking on. He cups my head, threading his fingers through my hair. He traces my mouth, lips, and tongue with his own. It's like he's trying to map every part of me.

My body arches against his. I can't get close enough to him.

His other hand finds my hip, his touch is rough and hot. He's branding me with his fingers, claiming me as his so I'm ruined for anyone else.

I try to tug my hands free, but his hold is too strong. With anyone else, it would make me panic but not with Logan. He's different than any other man I've known. He's gentle and kind but also strong when the moment calls for it.

I know without a doubt that I'm completely safe when I'm with him. He'd die before he'd let anything happen to me or Paisley. He hasn't said as much but it's there in the intensity of his gaze every time he looks at me.

Logan lifts his head, lust dancing in his expression. "Now, I'm playing to *my* strengths."

I squeeze my thighs together at his words and the rush of moisture they send into my panties. I've never wanted a man this way before. There's something about him that awakens a primal, animalistic side of me.

He groans and grinds against my body, his hardness poking me in the belly. "Since you cheated, I should be allowed compensation in the form of my choosing."

My heart is pounding so loudly that I'm sure he can hear it. I can only hope that his idea of compensation involves this man getting between my thighs and curing that ache. My voice comes out too breathy when I say, "That seems fair."

He nuzzles my neck, his beard tickling my sensitive skin. He licks and sucks, sending tingles all the way down to my clit. "Do you know what I want?"

"To torment me?" I gasp as the raging fire below my waist turns into an inferno. If he doesn't do something soon, I'm going to explode from the sheer force of my need.

He jerks his head back, staring at me with a frown. "Never to torment. Only to please."

His hold on my wrists has loosened so I press a hand to his cheek, cupping his face. "Then please me. I need you, Logan."

The moment I call his name, his expression transforms. Amusement has given way to masculine need and he drops my wrists. He yanks on the t-shirt, helping me out of it and tosses it beside us. The air from the nearby window floats in, cooling my skin and I shiver.

He quickly slams the window shut and turns his

attention back to me. "You're so damn beautiful lying in my floor with your breasts on display."

I've had men look at me with lust before and even comment on my body. It's a big part of working as a dancer. But with Logan, it's different. His words actually affect me, making me feel warm all over.

It's different with him because he's not just another paying customer, a dirty old man who wants to put his hands all over me. No, Logan cares about me. It's in the way he's done everything he can to make me feel safe and comfortable here, the way he's looked out for Paisley and taken us in without a second thought.

He leans down and puts his lips on my nipple, making a low growl that vibrates through me. His approval only adds to my arousal, making the place between my thighs grow slicker.

He alternates from breast to breast, giving each one his attention until I'm writhing against him. I can feel his erection with every push of my hips, and I wrap my legs around his waist. "Go lower."

He slips a hand under the barrier of the tiny boy shorts I'm wearing. His calloused fingers caress my slick, swollen mound and he instantly stills. "I need to see your pussy," his voice is low and urgent.

I give him a nod, unwilling to deny him anything.

When I give permission, he's yanking on the shorts and pulling them from my body. The sound he makes is part wonder and part anguish when he sees my bare pussy.

He reaches between his pants and cups himself. For a split second, he closes his eyes, and it makes me feel powerful to know that he's fighting for control. That the sight of my naked body is driving him to the edge.

He opens his eyes and meets my gaze. "This is my cream," he insists before he buries his face between my legs. He uses his tongue to tease me, lapping at my body.

His gentle motions and deep growls send me higher and higher. With every touch, he's showing me a different side to sex. One that doesn't take away from my pleasure but adds to it. One that doesn't leave me feeling dirty and used but treasured and cherished.

As the orgasm hits, I don't try to be quiet or hold back my ecstasy. I want Logan to know, to feel and understand that he's giving me a gift. He's made sex special for me. That's something I've never had before.

When he lifts his head, his face is glistening with my juices. "This is my favorite of your looks, when you're lying here nice and sated after I've just eaten you out."

I chuckle, my body still feeling as if I'm floating. I push myself into a sitting position and reach for his pants. After the scars he's shown me, I realize I've never seen him wear a belt nor did I see any in his closet. "My turn."

He puts his hands over mine. "Another night. This was about you."

His words make me pause. I've never had sex because I just wanted it. It's always been about a means to an end. A safe place to sleep for the night or a hot meal. Never about this, simply being taken care of by a man who puts me first.

"Are you sure?" I don't like the idea that he's not going to get a release. Not when he just so thoroughly satisfied me.

He cups my face, pushing the strands of hair from my eyes. "Every man in your life has used you, but I'm not them, Audrey. Your needs will always come before mine and right now, you don't want this. You just needed to get off."

"You're my husband, Logan. I don't expect something for nothing. I know I've lucked out where I am. You've been more than good to both me and Paisley."

He shakes his head, sadness creeping into his gaze. "And that's what kills me. If I touch you right now, you're going to think it's some type of trade. Your body in exchange for my protection and provision. But it won't be that to me at all." His thumb brushes against my lips. "It'll mean something."

My heart is pounding, and I want to ask him what exactly it'll mean to him. But I already feel like he's seen too much. Like he knows me, and I can't stand the feeling of exposure any longer. I step away from him. "Then I guess I'll head to bed."

He nods and I saunter to the door, intentionally putting a sway in my hips. I'm trying to get him to crack but even when I look back over my shoulder, his expression is still resolute. There will be no sex tonight.

IT'S HARD FOR ME TO SLEEP. I TOSS AND TURN, TRYING to understand Logan. He turned me down when he wanted my body. I saw the longing on his face, felt the way he grinded his hardness against me.

"The man makes no sense," I tell Paisley once she's had her morning bottle. He still didn't come to bed last night. I'd hoped he would at least join me in the big, king-size bed. But judging by the pillows and blanket on the couch, he slept there again.

I move to the nursery, figuring I'll get started on the next coat of paint. But it's already done. Not just the paint, the entire room. He's moved in all the furniture except the crib. There's a note on the rocking chair in his handwriting. I reach for it.

Audrey,

The second coat of paint should be dry by the time you read this. I'll be late tonight so I wanted to finish up. If Paisley needs anything else, I've left the keys to the truck and my credit card on the kitchen counter.

— Logan

I glance around the room, tears filling my eyes when I see that pink chandelier hanging from the ceiling. He is so intent on spoiling her. On spoiling both of us.

But I can't stay here. Eventually, my past will catch up with me and Paisley. We'll have to leave the handsome cowboy who makes my heart beat fast behind. It'll be easier to do that if I have a nest egg that I can use.

With that thought in mind, I move to the bedroom where I stored the list of clubs and bars around Courage County. *At least one of them has to be in need of a dancer, right?*

It takes most of the day but eventually, I manage to connect with a honkytonk bar in a neighboring town. The bartender won't make any promises over the phone, but he does say that I can come in and audition next week.

Despite what Logan said about not waiting up, I do anyway. I leave a plate of food warming for him in the oven. I never figured this is the kind of wife I'd be but I'm pretty excited about the possible job. The moment the bartender said I could audition, Logan was the first person I wanted to tell. I've never had someone I could share my good news with and that makes it even better.

When Logan stumbles up the back porch well past dark, he reeks of sweat and manure. He kicks off his boots and frowns at me. "You didn't have to wait."

"I have good news," I explain and beam at him. He'll be happy that I plan to contribute to the household. I'm not going to be someone mooching off his kindness. I'll help with the expenses.

He steps into the mudroom and strips down to his boxers. Despite how tired he looks, he gives me a big smile that makes his eyes crinkle at the corners. "Let me shower then I want to hear all about it."

By the time he's done in the shower, I've set his

food on the tiny table in the kitchen. The scene feels domestic and for a moment, I find myself wishing it could be real. Wishing it could always be like this.

His hair is still wet when he enters the kitchen, little water droplets clinging to it. He's wearing blue jeans and a white t-shirt with a long-sleeved plaid one layered over it. Only it's not buttoned up, just open. The sleeves are rolled up, showing off his strong forearms. Even though he looks dead on his feet, he doesn't immediately sit down and start eating. Instead, he gives me his full attention. "What's the big news?"

"I got an interview at the bar next week. They're looking for dancers. Can you believe it? I called fifteen different places before I found one that had an opening."

The delight I expected to see on Logan's face isn't there. "You're going back to stripping?"

8

AUDREY

"You're going back to stripping?" Logan demands once I've told him about my upcoming audition.

"I thought you'd be excited for me. I can help out with bills. I *need* this job, Logan." I never even finished high school. I have no education and I'm not qualified for anything, but this is something I can do.

He blows out a breath and ignores the food waiting for him on the table. He opens and closes his mouth, like he's searching for the words. Finally, he says, "I'll provide for you and for Paisley. You don't have to worry about anything. Your every need is now my responsibility to meet."

"I don't want to be your responsibility. I stand on my own two feet." He doesn't understand that the moment you lean on someone is the moment they disappear from your life.

"Well, I'm not letting you give lap dances to other cowboys." He steps closer to me, fire dancing in his eyes. I didn't take him for the jealous, possessive type. But despite the intense look on his face, I don't feel scared of him the way I did Calvin.

I take a step back and bump into the kitchen wall behind me. Craning my neck to look up at him, I say, "You'll have to get used to it."

"The hell I will," he mutters right before he puts his hands on the wall behind me. The simple motion cages me in, keeping me right where he wants me. Then he drops his head and kisses me. But this is different from last night's kiss. Last night's kiss was soft and explorative. This one is commanding and possessive.

There's the sound of a whimper and when I realize it was me, I put my hands against Logan's chest. I push him away and he breaks the kiss long enough to step back.

He still keeps his big hands on my hips, anchoring me to the spot. His chest is heaving and there's a wild look in his eyes, like a starving animal that just spotted prey. "I won't fuckin' share you, Audrey. You. Belong. To. Me."

Those four words are my undoing. I've never had anybody that was willing to claim me and even though this will never last, I pull him close again. I twine my arms around his neck and rub the short, prickly hairs there. "Show me. Show me that I'm yours."

He doesn't need to be asked twice. He slides his hands lower until he's clenching my ass. He picks me up then and I automatically wrap my legs around his hips. I rock against him, wringing a strangled groan from his throat. The one noise is all I need. He's as desperate for this moment as I am.

Logan carries me to the bedroom. As he lets me go, I pause to grind against him again. More moisture gathers in my panties and my nipples are so tight.

He pauses once, just long enough to glance into the crib and confirm that Paisley is still sleeping. When he's certain that she's fine, he shrugs out of his plaid button-up and his t-shirt is next.

I do the same, removing his t-shirt from my body. I already miss his masculine scent surrounding and marking me. I wore it all day, just waiting for the moment when he would come home and see me in it.

The appreciation in his gaze when I'm bare has me cupping my breasts. They're so heavy and full every time he looks at me. I pinch my nipples lightly, welcoming the sting of pain. "I ache for you."

"Dammit, Audrey." He crawls onto the bed. "Let me taste that sweet pussy. I've been thinking about it all day. I need to feel those pretty thighs clamping around my head again."

His words have me eagerly spreading my thighs. There's something about this man and the dirty things he says to me. It makes me wish I could be his woman. Only his woman.

I won't fuckin' share you, Audrey. You. Belong. To. Me.

I want that to be true forever. But since it can't, I'll take this moment. When I have to leave, I'll remember what it felt like to belong to Logan even if only for one night.

"Don't disappear on me now," he murmurs as he nudges me onto the pillows he's stacked up. His every thought is always about me. He's always trying to make me comfortable and take care of me. I can't help but wonder why. *What do you see that's worth protecting when no one else ever has?*

I don't want to think about those things. I don't want to focus on anything except Logan and his body, the pleasure it gives me and the pleasure I'm about to give him. That's all that matters tonight.

He puts a hand on my knee and pauses, clearly misunderstanding my sudden silence. "Do you still want this?"

I lean forward and press a kiss to his lips, nibbling on his plump lower one. He quickly takes control of the kiss, wrapping his hands around my head and angling me where he wants me.

By the time he pulls away, I'm leaning back against the pillows with my thighs spread. He grins. His eyes are hooded, and I wonder if he can see the same arousal on my face that I see on his.

He tugs on my panties. "I'm really not liking the barriers between us."

"Think I should wander around with no panties?" I tease.

He squeezes his cock and glares at me. "You do that, and I'll be between your thighs day and night."

I'd love nothing more than to spend my days and nights wrapped up with my cowboy husband in this tiny ranch home. We could spend hours exploring each other, making love until neither of us have any strength left. "I'm not sure that's much of a threat."

"That's because you don't understand a cowboy and his stamina," he promises as he ducks his head and licks my center. He laps up my juices, greedily drinking me in without letting me come. He's carefully avoiding my clit with each swipe of his tongue.

Finally, I tug on his hair, groaning in frustration. "Stop teasing me." I mean for the words to come out as a strong command but instead, they're a whimper. A begging declaration, announcing my need.

"All you had to do was ask."

Logan thrusts one of his thick digits into my aching channel before working his tongue across my clit. A shiver runs through me at the pleasure he's providing for my body. But it's not until he sucks my sensitive bud into his mouth that I clamp my thighs around his head.

One second before the release slams into me, I clap my hand over my mouth to keep from calling out his name and waking Paisley.

He brings me down for the orgasm gently, stroking me through it. I can't hear what he's saying as he presses kisses to the inside of my thighs. He's murmuring something under his breath with every feather-light touch of his lips to my skin.

"Was that your way of winning the argument?" I ask when I can finally think clearly again. If our arguments end this way, I'll be picking fights with this man every day.

He stands from the bed and yanks down his blue jeans to reveal his big cock. It's thicker and longer than anything I've ever seen. It's already glistening with moisture and he tugs on it twice before crawling back onto the bed. "No, this isn't the way I settle an argument."

His thick cock nudges my slick folds, and I can't hold back a groan.

"Maybe it should be." I spread my legs, bracing my feet against the mattress. I've never wanted sex the way I do with this man. He makes me feel things and when we're together, it's not just about the physical. There's something deeper, something I can't even put into words.

He thrusts inside my body, his broad head pushing deep into my channel. He stills before whispering a profanity. "I forgot a condom."

I wait for a rush of panic at his words, but I don't feel one. Maybe because I like the idea of carrying

his baby, the idea of giving our daughter a sister. "It's
fine. I'm clean."

"Me too," he reassures. "Pregnancy?"

"Wrong time of the month," I say. Maybe I
imagine it, but I think disappointment flickers
across his face. I have to be reading that wrong. It
has to be relief I'm seeing.

He cups my face, looking deep into my eyes. It's
like he's trying to memorize this moment as he starts
pumping his hips. Every time he rocks into me,
there's the most delicious friction. He fills me so
completely and so fully that it feels like we were
always meant to be this way.

"You feel so good," he murmurs. The wonder and
amazement in his voice are telling me this isn't just
magical for me. It's special for him too.

"Can you come for me again?" He reaches
between our bodies, playing with my clit. His fingers
are rough, but his touch is gentle. With every sure
swipe of his fingers, I move closer and closer to the
edge.

When I do come with a cry of ecstasy, he presses
a kiss to my lips to silence me. He absorbs my pleasure, groaning his back into me. I feel the moment
he comes, the way his release shoots deep inside of

me. For one wild second, all I can do is hope we made a baby together.

After his orgasm, he collapses onto the bed beside me. His chest rises and falls rapidly. I want to touch him again, to feel his arms around me. But I don't know what to do next.

He seems to sense my debate because he holds me, pulling me on top of his body. We're sticky and sweaty and even though he just came, he's still hard between my thighs.

I run my hand along his side, over the scars. A scared little boy grew into such a strong man. One that is kind and gentle and protective. One that I wish I could stay with forever.

Life feels simpler, easier here with Logan. There's a part of me that wants to lean into that feeling, to simply let him become my strength. I know better than that. Even if he wanted to keep both of us, my past is going to show up one day.

"Audrey," he calls my name softly and touches my hair. He brushes it away from my face before saying, "I know you're running from something. You can tell me about it."

I can still feel Calvin's sticky blood drying on my skin. If I tell Logan anything, it makes him an accomplice. I may not be able to do much, but I can protect him. "I'm a big girl. My problems are my own."

"You're married to me. That means your problems are mine now too," he argues.

I wish things could be that simple. I wish I could tell Logan everything and let him help me. But no one can help me now. I went too far and I'm on my own. The best thing I can do for him is leave soon.

9

LOGAN

I'VE SLEPT IN MY BED WITH AUDREY ALL NIGHT. SHE'S not a sound sleeper though. She often kicks and groans. She tosses and turns, murmuring incoherently in her sleep. I hate that she's being tormented by something I can't see.

As her husband, I want to charge in and rescue her from the monsters that put those shadows in her eyes. But I can't fight what I don't know and what she won't show me. I'll have to work harder to win her trust. I almost thought we were getting somewhere last night but she shut me out again.

Paisley stirs in her crib and I leave the warmth of the bed to check on the little girl. She stares up at me, her gaze sleepy. I make a quick diaper change before I take her to the kitchen where I warm a bottle.

"You're daddy's sweet little girl, aren't you?" I ask as I feed her. I can't imagine not having her and Audrey in my life. They're my whole world now and I'll do whatever it takes to protect them both.

"I'll make you a promise," I say when I pull the bottle away long enough to burp her. I look into these deep blue eyes, feeling my heart swell. "I'll always be there for you. From your first day of school to your first dance, even your first heart-break, I'll have your back. I'll teach you how to build a tree fort and drive a tractor and take you fishing. You can count on your old man."

She grins up at me as if she understands the full weight of my words, and I can only hope that she does. Because Paisley Jolene is my daughter and she's got a father she can depend on.

Audrey

"You're daddy's sweet little girl, aren't you?" I listen to Logan's soft tenor as he croons over my baby girl. I don't think he realized that the baby monitor is on in there.

I listen to the solemn promises he makes her, my eyes filling with tears. He's everything a mother could want for her baby. In this moment, I realize I can't leave him. I'll do whatever it takes to keep Paisley close to him, to have her grow up around this kind of love and acceptance. Maybe in time he'll even start to love me too.

Decision made, I leave the bed and move to the bathroom. After I handle my business and brush my teeth, I start the shower water. There's a knock on the door before Logan comes inside.

"Is Paisley settled?" I ask even as my heart lurches at the sight of him, all messy bedhead and tired gaze. I don't know how or when, but this man became the other half of my heart.

"She's in the crib, cuddling her giraffe. Well, chewing on him." He shrugs. "The internet says it's normal that she wants to chew on things and not a sign that she's hungry. I checked the packaging of the toy and it's made of silicone. It's BPA-free and contains no—"

I lean up and press a kiss to his lips. He's adorable, the way he's always worried about her. I can already tell that I'm going to spend most of Paisley's childhood reassuring him that she's healthy and happy.

"You're smiling this morning," he remarks when I step away from him.

I tug off my clothes until I'm standing naked in front of my husband. "I'm *very* happy this morning. Now, let's do our part for the environment and conserve water."

"Hell yeah, we will." He tugs off his clothes but stops when he's left with his boxers and disappears from the room. He returns a moment later with the baby video monitor. He places it on the bathroom counter, so we'll be able to hear and see Paisley.

Three delicious orgasms later, I'm cleaner than I've ever been. Or maybe it's dirtier. I really don't care. All I know is that I'm flying high with the knowledge that Paisley and I belong here with this cowboy.

He watches me dry my hair with the blower and when I reach for my brush, Logan takes it from my hands. We're standing in front of the mirror and there's something oddly intimate about having him brush my hair for me.

I close my eyes and lean into his touch. "About last night, I still need to earn my own money. I know you want to provide for us but it's not that easy for me."

He sighs but doesn't stop brushing my hair. "I'm not against you having a job. I'm against you having a job that involves stripping down so other men can see your beautiful body. I want that for myself and I don't give a damn if it makes me selfish or old-fashioned."

"I wouldn't want you to have a job where you were stripping down for other women," I admit, seeing his point on that. It would drive me insane to know they were looking at my man and lusting after him. Maybe there are some women that are secure enough to handle that but I'm not one of them. "I'll look for a job as a waitress or something."

I won't make as much money that way, but I'm not planning to leave Logan anymore. I'll just hope I get lucky and that my past doesn't catch up with me again.

"I'd rather be the sole provider for our family. But I'll support whatever you want to do," he says as he presses a gentle kiss to my shoulder.

I can't help smiling again. "You said our family."

"Our family," he repeats again softly.

I love the sound of that but before I can tell him

this, his phone rings on the bathroom counter. He glances at the number. "That's Sheriff Luke."

This can't be happening. I just decided to stay here. He called us his family. Our lives were finally turning around.

"Hey, Luke. How's your family?" Logan listens for a moment, grinning the entire time. He's so relaxed that it makes me wonder if I misunderstood the situation. "Yeah, you and Austin should come by for dinner next week. Luke Jr. can meet our Paisley."

I'm standing close enough that I can hear Luke's side of the conversation too. "We'll do that. Listen, we got a situation down at the station. You reckon you and the Missus could swing by in a few minutes?"

Logan looks to me.

I tap my wrist in the area where I'd wear a watch and mouth for two hours. That's enough time to get a head start. I won't tell Logan where I'm headed. Then he won't have to lie to the sheriff.

"I'll need about two hours. Does that work for you? Alright, thanks, Sheriff. See ya then." He ends the call and focuses on me. "What's wrong?"

I shake my head and pull my now dry hair into a ponytail. "Clothes. I need clothes."

Dazed, I move to the bedroom and start going

through the dresser where I put away my t-shirts. "I can't believe I unpacked clothes like I would get to stay here. I really did lose my mind this time."

"Why wouldn't you get to stay? What are you talking about?"

Logan's confusion breaks through my shock. I have to stop and think clearly. I have to be strong for him. He's been so good to us.

I slip into a pair of panties and a bra. Then I layer a t-shirt with a skull design over it and pull on some dark wash blue jeans. When I'm finally dressed, I turn my attention back to my husband.

He's changed into pants, but he hasn't covered his chest with a shirt yet. That beautiful chest that I kissed my way across this morning in the shower before dropping to my knees.

I take a deep breath and force myself not to relive those moments with him. We made so many beautiful memories together. "Look, you have to go see the sheriff by yourself, and it's better if you don't ask me any questions."

Understanding crosses his features. "This is about what you're running from."

Without answering him, I grab my bag. I start shoving Paisley's clothes from the drawer in there first. I can get by on an outfit or two, but she matters the most. She'll always matter the most.

"Audrey."

I don't answer him or even look up from what I'm doing. *Every minute counts now.*

"Audrey," he calls my name louder this time as if an increase in volume will somehow change this. I made a stupid decision one night and now the three of us will never get to be a family.

Ignoring Logan, I stay focused on the task. At least, I do until I feel his strong hands on my shoulders.

"Talk to me, dammit."

I look up only to realize he's blurry. I swipe at my face, hating the tears that mean I let myself care. I got attached. Even worse, I let Paisley get attached. There's no way she's not going to feel the loss of this strong cowboy who was willing to be her father.

"If I tell you, you're an accomplice," I warn. I expect that will be enough and he'll let me go. Cowboys like him don't belong in the middle of trouble like this. As it is, he already got more than he bargained for when I showed up with my little baby girl.

He tugs me to the bed, helping me sit down. Then he kneels in front of it and lifts my chin. In a solemn tone, he says, "I don't care what it makes me. Tell me everything."

I stare at my lap where I've clenched my hands. A tear drop runs down my cheek as I whisper, "I killed a man."

10

AUDREY

I hear Logan's sharp inhale, but he doesn't say anything else, so I let the whole story tumble out. I'm so tired of keeping it inside anyway. "Calvin was one of my regulars at the club. He seemed normal at first. There weren't any red flags or warning signs."

I've spent so many nights trying to figure out what I didn't see. Monsters aren't supposed to look like us. They're supposed to be ugly with fangs. They shouldn't wear cheap business suits and act like everyday people.

"Then he started leaving gifts for me in my dressing room, in my car. I tried to let him down gently. I told him that I didn't really have time for a relationship." At that point, I still thought he was a nice, normal guy.

"He didn't listen, did he?" There's an unmistakable note of anger in Logan's voice when he speaks.

I glance up but from his expression, I don't think I'm the one he's angry with. "Then the gifts started appearing in my apartment. I would come home from work and they would just be there. I went to the police. But according to the officer I spoke with, I should have been flattered by the attention."

Logan swears under his breath. I'm not sure what he said exactly, but I think he just threatened the cop I talked to.

"He started following me after that. I couldn't even go to the grocery store and talk to the bagger without Calvin flying into a rage." I squeeze my eyes shut. The owner of the club had banned Calvin from the premise. But by that point, nothing was getting through to him.

"The police *still* wouldn't do anything?" I can hear the mounting frustration in Logan's tone. I wonder how different the story would have played out if Logan had been in my life back then. I know he would have intervened. He's not the type that would have sat on the sidelines while I was stalked and harassed.

"Calvin was the manager of the office supply store his father owned. He was married with two teenage daughters and he went to church. He made it out like I was this hysterical woman who was fixated on *him*."

Since then, I've learned abusers often do this. They torment you until you're scared out of your mind then act normal in front of everyone else. You're left looking crazy while everyone believes him.

"He showed up at my place late one night. He insisted that I was going away with him to his cabin in the woods." I still remember the feeling in my gut when he pushed through the flimsy locks and burst into the apartment. Some part of me knew in that moment that I would need to fight my way out.

"I tried to talk to him calmly. Tell him I wasn't going to go," my voice drops lower with each word. There are so many details about that night and all of them are trying to come back at once. They're scattered fragments, puzzle pieces that belong together, that tell the story of a scared young mom.

Paisley grunts from her crib and that's when the tears come again. "She saw it, Logan. She saw me stab Calvin. I didn't mean to. We were in my kitchen and he reached for her and I can't even tell you why I did it. I just reacted."

"Look at me." He puts a hand under my chin and

tilts my face up so I'm staring into his eyes. "Your mother's instincts told you that Calvin was danger-ous. He reached for your baby and you defended her."

"There was so much blood. I don't think he survived. You don't think he did, do you?" It wakes me up in the middle of the night, the cold fear that Calvin could come back for us. But I'm also terrified he's dead. I don't know which fear torments me more.

"It doesn't matter." He pushes a strand of hair that escaped my ponytail from my face. "Whether he's dead or alive, Calvin is never going to hurt you again. Now, walk me through it."

"What?" I frown at him.

He takes my hand and tugs me to my feet. "Walk me through everything that happened. I'll be Calvin. Just show me what you did."

I do what he said, not sure why it matters. Maybe he just didn't understand my earlier explanation. But when we're done, he wants me to go through it again. This time I'm Calvin.

"Now you understand why I have to leave," I tell him. We've taken almost an hour together. But he has to go to the sheriff's office and I need to get on the road.

"You're not leaving," he confidently declares. "We'll face this together then you and Paisley will be free."

"You can't just promise me something like that," I argue as I hold my little girl close. She's the most precious thing in the world to me. She and my cowboy husband.

"Do you trust me to be the husband you want and the father that Paisley needs?" He asks, his tone gentle. There's something in his gaze. I can feel the way he's thinking things through, coming up with a plan.

I don't hesitate. "Yes."

"Then let me help you and after today, we'll be free to focus on our family," he says, pressing a kiss to my forehead.

THE NEXT HOUR PASSES BY IN A BLUR. WE DROP Paisley off at Logan's brother's house. I meet Ranger and his wife briefly. They're both nice to me and they seem delighted to have the chance to babysit their new niece. They took to her as if she'd been born into the family.

When we walk into the Courage County Police Department, my legs nearly give out and I stumble.

Logan wraps an arm around my waist and presses a gentle kiss to my ear. "It's going to be OK. All you have to do is trust me."

The building is only a couple of rooms and two jail cells. The strange thing about it is how many bouquets of flowers there are everywhere. Every possible surface seems to have flowers on it. The sheriff here is clearly obsessed.

Logan sees me looking and explains, "Luke's wife is Austin. She owns Bloom Anywhere, the florist shop in town."

A tall cowboy with a haunted look in his gaze leaves the sheriff's office and for a moment I assume he's Luke. But then Logan greets him warmly and welcomes him back to town.

"Who was that?" I ask when the man leaves.

"That was Deputy Griffin. He's come back after years away," Logan says and gestures for me to take a seat in one of the chairs outside the office.

I take the seat and wait while he makes a cup of coffee. He passes it to me then sits in the metal chair next to mine.

I sip the warm beverage, surprised at how much

it calms my nerves just to have something in my hands. Logan must have sensed that somehow. "Why did he leave?"

"He was just a kid when his father killed his mom. His aunt raised him after that. But I don't envy him, growing up in a small town where everybody knows your story. It's not easy to heal from that kind of pain without some distance."

My heart hurts for Griffin. "I hope he found what he needed while he was away."

He takes my hand and gives it a gentle squeeze. "Me too."

Not long after that, Sheriff Luke finally comes to get us. He's not like I expected. He's young and blonde though his hair is already graying around the temples. Exhaustion is evident on his face, but he still gives me a warm smile.

I wait for him to lead us back to some small interrogation room for this, but he doesn't. He ushers us into his office and points to the chairs. "Sorry 'bout the heat, y'all. County doesn't have the funds to fix the HVAC so you're just going to have to freeze your asses off." He grimaces and looks to me. "Pardon the expression."

When he settles in his chair, he opens his mouth.

But I already know what he's going to say and I'm tired of being scared. I'm tired of waiting for this awful, horrible thing to happen. "I'm ready to confess."

He quirks an eyebrow.

"I stabbed—"

"She means me," Logan quickly interjects. He tells Luke everything that happened as if he were the one who stabbed Calvin. I try to stop him. I keep interrupting but each time, Logan squeezes my hand and continues with the story.

By the time the confession is over, the sheriff is looking between us as if he doesn't know what to make of it all. "Well, gotta be honest here, Logan. I was calling to let you know you were right. Sticky did take your Gator like you thought. The sheriff in Sweetgrass caught him trying to sell it. Course now, I gotta make some calls and ask questions about this situation. Y'all sit tight."

The moment he's gone, I push to my feet and glare at Logan. "What did you just do?"

He shrugs, looking unconcerned. "I told you I'd take care of it."

"By lying to Luke?" Now we're going to be in trouble for lying to the cops on top of everything else. I don't see a way for this to end well.

"Keep your voice down," Logan says.

"You can't just do this," my voice comes out as a desperate plea. I don't want to lose Logan, not after I just found him.

"I told you that I will protect you and Paisley. Whatever happens now, let it fall on me. I'm strong enough to take it."

"You weren't even in Miami that night," I point out.

He's quiet for a moment as if he's choosing his words carefully. "One of my brothers has enough influence and money to place me at the scene. No questions asked. They'll never even need to interview you. You and Paisley will be kept completely safe."

I cross the room to sit in his lap and wrap my arms around his broad shoulders. I don't care that I'm straddling him in the middle of the sheriff's office. Inhaling deeply, I bury my face in his coat. "I'm scared to lose you."

He rubs my back in a soothing motion. "You won't lose me, I promise. Whatever happens, I'll deal with the fallout then we'll be free to be together."

I don't know how long we stay wrapped up like this, just holding each other. But eventually, Luke comes back into his office, and I let go of Logan. I

take my seat beside him and he squeezes my hand
again, giving me a nod.

Luke takes a seat behind his desk and shakes his
head. "So, you're confessing to stabbing a man
named Calvin about six weeks ago in her apartment,
is that correct?"

"Yes, Sheriff," Logan answers without a hint of
nervousness in his voice. I don't know how he's
finding the strength to stay so calm but I'm grateful
for it.

"Well, I found Calvin. It seems he died about a
week later on account of his wife came home early
and caught him in bed with their marriage
counselor."

"You're making this shit up," Logan says, leaning
forward.

Luke barks out a laugh. "I didn't believe it either.
Got the report sent over and everything. That man is
dead and gone. Had a nice knife wound that his wife
sewed up. Apparently, he told her he'd been mugged,
but he didn't want to go to the hospital. That's when
she got suspicious."

Logan makes a frustrated noise. "He knew he'd
been doing something wrong."

"You reap what you sow," Luke agrees. "Now, you
ready to deal with your Gator?"

The men start discussing Logan's stolen property while I'm left to absorb their words. Calvin is dead. He's gone. He can't ever come for me or Paisley again. We're finally free, just like Logan promised.

As we stand to leave, Luke scowls. "Sorry, you had to come all this way out, Audrey. My wife thought she would be popping in, but the morning sickness got her again. She really wanted to meet you."

"That's why you called for both of us?" I ask, feeling more relief course through me. I'd automatically assumed he knew something and I was in trouble.

Luke walks us out to Logan's truck. "She runs the flower shop around here and she knows you're looking for a job. With our second son coming, she'll be needing the extra help soon."

"She knew I was looking for a job?" I repeat.

"Small town," Logan explains before glancing at Luke. "She's still used to Miami."

"Well, we're glad to have you here." He tips his hat to me then turns to Logan. He claps him on the shoulder. "Don't be making confessions."

"It's my last one," Logan promises.

BY THE TIME WE PICK UP PAISLEY FROM RANGER AND his wife, it's dinner time. They insist on having us stay over and we eat a meal together. Tia is sweet and welcoming, everything I'd want in a sister-in-law.

She's different from me. I think maybe she grew up in church or something because she has this wide-eyed innocence that suggests she's been sheltered. Still, she's accepting and kind. She tells me she'll babysit anytime I need the help.

When we're back at Logan's place, I feel so exhausted that I could collapse. Instead, I give Paisley her last bottle of the night and settle her into her crib. Watching her sleep, a shiver runs down my spine. I thought I was going to lose everything today.

"Hey," Logan says the word softly as his arms encircle me. He holds me up, keeping me from collapsing onto the floor. He presses soft kisses to my temple, the side of my face, and my neck. "I got you, Mama. Tell me what's going on."

"I can't believe it's over. It's done." The whole day is so surreal, like a blissful dream where the monster is finally vanquished and now I can live forever with my handsome prince. "Is it really over?"

"It's over," he reassures me as he sets me on the

bed. He pulls off my clothes until I'm only left in my underwear. His clothes are next, and I expect he's going to make love to me. But he doesn't. He pulls me under the covers and wraps his arms around me, spooning me from behind. "You were so brave today. You faced the nightmare and came out on the other side."

I turn in his arms, needing to see his face. "You were willing to go to prison for me."

No one has ever defended me like that before. I've never had someone stand up for me and protect me, to be willing to sacrifice themselves without a second thought. This man was ready to lose everything for me. His reputation, his standing in the community, even his freedom. He didn't blink or hesitate.

"Why?" I think I know the answer, but I want the words. I crave them tonight.

"I love you," he says. "I love you and Paisley. I told you that you will always come before me and I meant that. No matter what happens in our lives, if there is a sacrifice to be made, it will be my honor to be the one to make it. You and Paisley are my world now."

"I love you back," I whisper, feeling the tears

stream down my cheeks. I never knew it was possible to be this happy or feel this loved. It's been a hard, dark road to my cowboy. But he was worth every minute of the journey.

11

LOGAN

Waking up beside my wife is something I could get used to. She spent last night between tears and relief. She's been carrying this burden for so long. I can only imagine how heavy that must have been. But she's no longer alone. Now she has me to shoulder her pain.

"Hi," she murmurs sleepily when she opens her eyes. I love that half-lidded, groggy expression. She looked so peaceful when she finally drifted to sleep in my arms an hour ago. I'll stay up all night with her if it chases her monsters away.

"Hi," I whisper back.

Paisley grunts between us as if reminding us she's here. I never pictured myself becoming an instant dad. But the moment I laid eyes on this precious little girl I knew I was in love with her. She's perfect, just like her pretty mama.

"Hi to you too," Audrey says, peering down at our little one. She puts a hand on her daughter's rounded belly that's full thanks to the bottle I gave her a few minutes ago.

Her daughter grins up at her and kicks out her legs in excitement. I love watching her interact with us. I can't wait until she's talking and telling us everything she thinks and feels.

Audrey laughs. "Someone is chipper this morning."

"That's because Daddy promised to show her and Mama around the farm," I explain.

"Daddy," She repeats the word softly before glancing up at me. Tears are shimmering in her gaze. "I like it when you say that."

I take a deep breath and admit what I've been thinking about all night long, "I want to legally adopt her. I want Paisley Jolene to be mine in every way, just like you are."

Audrey

MY HEART FEELS LIKE IT MIGHT JUST BURST FROM happiness at Logan's words. He wants to adopt Paisley. He plans to become her father.

He continues, "I looked into it and it's considered paternity fraud if we just add my name to the birth certificate. Besides if her biological dad ever comes back into her life, I'd want him to be able to claim her too."

"That's probably a long shot," I warn him. I've searched a hundred times, trying to locate the man. It hurts my heart that he has a child out in the world and doesn't know it. He won't get to watch her grow up and be part of Paisley's life. But at the same time, I'm glad she has Logan. He'll love her just as deeply as if she were biologically his.

I reach for his hand and squeeze it. "If we never find him, she's already the luckiest little girl in the world because she has an amazing adoptive dad."

He looks down at our little girl who's making the cutest baby babbling sounds. "What do you think, Paisley Jolene? Are you ready to become an official Scott?"

She grins up at him before sticking her whole hand in her mouth.

"I'm pretty sure that was a yes," I tell him right before I kiss my sexy husband again.

AFTER A LAZY MORNING TOGETHER, THE THREE OF US are about to leave to see the farm. I'm excited that Logan plans to show us around. But the moment we're on the porch, one of the Gators pulls to a stop in our front yard.

Ethan hops out and sprints across the lawn that's covered in a mixture of ice and snow. He stops at the bottom of the steps. "I'm supposed to pick up my wife today, but my damn SUV won't start. Loan me the keys to your truck."

"I told you not to buy that gas-guzzling piece of shit," Logan chastises as he pulls his keys from his pocket. He tosses them to his brother.

Ethan scowls at him for the lecture and catches the keys mid-air. He's already jogging toward the garage when I call after him, "Good luck, Ethan."

He pauses long enough to turn to me and gives me a slight nod. "Thanks. I think I'm going to need it."

"Will he be OK?" I ask as Logan's truck pulls from the drive.

"Truthfully, I don't know," Logan answers. "He was married once before, and it wasn't a good one. I don't imagine the second one will be any easier on him."

"Maybe he'll get a nice woman," I say, hopeful for him. Sure, Ethan wasn't all that friendly when I met him at the chapel for the wedding. But I can appreciate the fact that he was feeling protective over his brother.

"I hope so," Logan answers, putting an arm around me. "Now, come here. I want to show you this first."

I pause to adjust the straps of the baby carrier on my shoulders. This was another one of Logan's purchases that I'm glad for. Being able to have Paisley against my chest while still being hands-free is great.

Logan leads me to the backyard and gestures at a tree that's about twenty feet from the house. It has no leaves on the thick branches and it's covered in a light coating of ice.

"We have trees in Miami," I say slowly, teasing him.

"Not like this." He puffs out his chest and pats the tree's trunk. "This beauty is where Paisley and I will build her first tree house. You should see it in the spring when the leaves are nice and full."

"She'll love that," I answer, my heart warming at the thought.

He gestures around the property. "There's a lake about twenty feet away from us and the moment the weather is warm, she's getting swimming lessons."

I can't help but laugh at how serious he's being. He's taken to fatherhood like he's made for it. "You have this all figured out."

"I want her to be happy here," he says softly.

"Dada," she squeals.

We both freeze, exchanging a look before Logan lets out a whoop and bends so he's eye-level with her. "Damn right, baby girl. I'm your dada."

"You've been working with her," I pretend to pout.

"In my defense, I did encourage her to say mama too. I can't help it if she picked a favorite." The boyish grin on his face and the way his eyes are sparkling have me leaning in to press a kiss to his lips.

"You're my favorite too," I promise when I pull away.

Logan and I spend the rest of the day on the family ranch. It's so big and vast that he still doesn't get to show me everything. But what he has shared takes my breath away. This place is beautiful. It's a piece of untouched paradise tucked away in the mountains. I can't wait to spend the rest of my days here, raising my little family with the cowboy I love.

EPILOGUE

LOGAN

"Mommy," Paisley calls from the backseat. My little girl's vocabulary is growing by leaps and bounds every day. But that's her favorite word. Not that I can blame her. Paisley's mom does happen to be the most special woman in the whole world.

"Soon," I promise her.

She sticks her lower lip out. "Now!"

That's probably her second favorite word followed by "no" and "ice keen". I'm pretty sure that "Dada" ranks in the top twenty. Possibly. It's hard to tell with a one-year-old.

The last six months have been the best of my life. Just when I think our lives can't get any better, they suddenly do. Like when Audrey got her GED last month. The three of us celebrated with ice cream sandwiches at Ernie's diner.

She's applying to colleges in the state now. While she'll take online classes if she has to, I know her dream is to go to a brick-and-mortar school. I'll support that dream no matter what it takes.

I've already started pricing apartments around her top three schools. We figure we'll try to get her on a part-time schedule that lets her attend school three to four days a week. We'll spend the remaining days on the ranch.

My brothers have already made it clear that they're willing to do anything to help Audrey. That means they'll tough it out for the four or so years without my full-time help until we can get back to living on the ranch permanently.

Audrey wants to work in the foster care system. She said that because of her history and mine, she wants to be there for other kids. We've talked about becoming foster parents ourselves when Paisley is older and we're ready to expand our family. But for now, the little girl that's made from sunshine and giggles keeps us both on our toes.

I pull into the parking lot for Bloom Anywhere and take Paisley in my arms. My wife works part-time here now. I keep telling her that she doesn't have to worry about earning money, but I under-stand what this is. She's a survivor and that need to prepare for the worst may never fully leave her.

"Mommy!" My daughter squeals just as Audrey exits the building. She practically floats across the street.

She's looking like a goddess this afternoon. She's dressed in her tight, cut-off blue jeans and a black halter top that makes me think about last night. She gave me a lap dance that I'll always remember. Even if we have seven decades together, I'll never get enough of this woman. I'll crave her touch forever.

She bounds into the truck, her cheeks flushed from the afternoon sun. She covers our daughter with kisses. "My baby girl!"

I love the easy affection between the two of them. She reads so many books on motherhood. She's terrified of being a bad mom, of not being there for Paisley the way her mom wasn't there for her. But on those nights when her fears are loud, I remind her of how incredible she is. I point out that Paisley looks at her like she hung the moon.

"My turn," I playfully grumble and kiss Paisley's other chubby cheek. The little girl dissolves into delighted squeals that have me and Audrey quickly joining in.

"Ice keen, Dada!" Paisley finally demands when I've settled her back into her car seat and started the truck again.

Audrey glares at me. "Did you promise her again?"

"It's not my fault that the girl has never met a vegetable she likes," I argue. Like me, Paisley likes potatoes in all forms but will reject any other vegetable that touches her plate. Audrey spends half of her time trying to sneak green things into our meals. Last week, she even made something called kale cookies.

To get Paisley to eat green foods, I have to bribe her with ice cream sandwiches. Those are her favorite. Mine too.

"What happens when she's twenty and you're not here to give her ice cream?" Audrey asks as I turn into the parking lot for Ernie's diner. Griffin, the sheriff's deputy, wasted no time when he came home. He put a ring on the finger of Missy, one of the waitresses that works here.

"Why would she not be here?" I ask as I unbuckle our little girl. I toss her up into the air in the way that makes her laugh. "You're never leaving Daddy, are you?"

"She's going to eventually go," Audrey says,

giving me that soft-eyed look she has when she thinks I'm being an overprotective father.

"We're a no to that one, aren't we?" I ask.

Paisley grins at me, revealing even more of those little baby teeth. I never thought babies were that cute until Paisley. Now I have the world's cutest one, and she's all mine. "Ice keen!"

"See, I know how to keep this sweet girl around," I smile triumphantly at Audrey who just shakes her head and follows me into Ernie's.

After the ice cream, we drive back to the ranch. I roll down the window to wave at Ethan and his wife, Valentine.

I wasn't sure that Ethan's marriage would make it since his first one was such a train wreck. But he's so happy with Valentine. He spoils her constantly and she looks at him like he's a superhero. I know what that's like because I get that same look from Audrey. It makes me feel like there isn't anything I can't do.

The happy couple waves at us as we continue up the drive to our house. Since my girls have moved in, the house has seen all sorts of improvements. Flowers up the walk and the driveway has been paved.

There are rocking chairs on the front porch now and a tiny pink bike in the front yard. Paisley still doesn't fully understand the concept of the bike yet so mainly she just sits in the seat while I push her around. But I don't mind. I cherish every minute with my daughter.

Since it's hot today, we take her to the lake on our property. She's learned how to float though that doesn't exactly ease my mind. I know it's only one-part of swim safety and the moment she's old enough to grasp the basic movements, I'll have this girl swimming.

It's funny the things I never worried about before Paisley. Now I think about everything. Audrey fusses at me sometimes for overthinking it. She says I worry about her because my own childhood was so hard. But I don't think that's it. I think it's just that there's so much love in my heart for this little girl and her sweet mama.

After she's splashed her heart out and her eyes are growing heavy, I settle Paisley on the picnic blanket between me and Audrey. She's reading a book, some romance if I had to guess by the way she kept looking at me while I was in the water.

I stretch out on the blanket and stare up at the sky, reaching for Audrey's hand. The familiar zing of attraction still goes through my body at just her touch.

"What are you thinking?" She asks after the comfortable silence has stretched between us.

I let out a soft sigh. "I'm thinking that my life is perfect these days."

She chuckles and scoots Paisley closer to me so she can put her head on my shoulder. "I think our lives are perfect too."

When I first heard about my grandfather's plan to force me and my brothers to marry, I was so angry at him. But now I hope he's looking down on me. I hope he sees Audrey and Paisley and how special they are. He sent this cowboy a family, and I couldn't be happier.

READ NEXT: THE COWBOY'S VALENTINE

I'm a grumpy loner cowboy and I like it that way. Until my beautiful mail order bride arrives and suddenly, I want more than a marriage in name only.

Ethan

I'm not exactly Mr. Hearts and Flowers. I mean, I was at one point in my life. Back before I discovered my wife was cheating on me in front of the whole town. Oh, and the baby she was carrying wasn't even mine.

So, to say that my late grandfather insisting that marriage is a requirement for claiming my rightful inheritance doesn't exactly have me jumping for joy.

But it's too late because my mail order bride is already on her way.

I have every intention of making this marriage in name only. Should be simple and easy enough…until I lay eyes on Valentine. She's the prettiest thing I've ever seen and I'm instantly in love. But are the scars from my past too much for a ray of sunshine like her?

Valentine

Yep, I was born on Valentine's Day and yeah, it is a dorky name. But that doesn't mean that I can't believe in family and love and forever. Sure, I was a foster kid who never knew those things.

But I want to. That's why I signed up to be a mail order bride.

Looking at Ethan, I know that we can make this work if he'll just give me a chance. He seems determined to close himself off, but maybe for the first time, I can convince someone I'm worth keeping.

Will this lonely cowboy finally let me inside? Or are we doomed to keep this as a marriage in name only?

If you love a mail order bride romance with a grumpy cowboy who falls for a sunshine woman, then it's time to meet Ethan in The Cowboy's Valentine.

Read Ethan and Valentine's Story

Welcome to Courage County where protective alpha heroes fall for strong curvy women they love and defend. There's NO cheating and NO cliffhangers. Just a sweet, sexy HEA in each book.

Love on the Ranch

Her Alpha Cowboy

Pregnant and alone, Riley has nowhere to go until the alpha cowboy finds her. Will she fall in love with her rescuer?

Her Older Cowboy

Summer is making a baby with her brother's best friend. But he insists on making it the old-fashioned way.

Her Protector Cowboy

Jack will do whatever it takes to protect his curvy woman after their hot one-night stand...then he plans to claim her!

Her Forever Cowboy

Dean is in love with his best friend's widow. When they're stranded together for the night, will he finally tell her how he feels?

Her Dirty Cowboy

The ranch's newest hire also happens to be the woman Adam had a one-night stand with...and she's carrying his baby!

Her Sexy Cowboy

She's a scared runaway with a baby. He's determined to protect them both. But neither of them expected to fall in love.

Her Wild Cowboy

He'll keep his curvy woman safe, even if it means a marriage in name only. But what happens when he wants to make it a real marriage?

Her Wicked Cowboy

One hot night with Jake gave me the best gift of my life: a beautiful baby girl. Will he want us to be a family when I show up on his doorstep a year later?

Courage County Brides

The Cowboy's Bride

The only way out of my horrible life is to become a mail order bride. But will my new cowboy husband be willing to take a chance on love?

The Cowboy's Soulmate

Can a jaded playboy find forever with his curvy mail order bride and her baby? Or will her secret ruin their future?

The Cowboy's Valentine

I'm a grumpy loner cowboy and I like it that way. Until my beautiful mail order bride arrives and suddenly, I want more than a marriage in name only.

The Cowboy's Match

Will this mail order bride matchmaker take a chance on love when she falls for the bearded cowboy who happens to be her VIP client?

The Cowboy's Obsession

Can this stalker cowboy show the curvy schoolteacher that he's the one for her?

The Cowboy's Sweetheart

Rule #1 of becoming a mail order bride: never fall in love with your cowboy groom.

The Cowboy's Angel

Can this cowboy single dad with a baby find love with his new mail order bride?

The Cowboy's Heiress

This innocent heiress is posing as a mail order bride. But what happens when her grumpy cowboy husband discovers who she really is?

Courage County Warriors

Rescue Me

Getting out was hard. Knowing who to trust was easy: my dad's best friend. He's the only man I can count on, but will we be able to keep our hands off each other?

Protect Me

When I need a warrior to protect me, I know just who to turn to: my brother's best friend. But will this grumpy cowboy who's guarding my body break my heart?

Shield Me

When trouble comes for me, I know who to call—
my ex-boyfriend's dad. He's the only one who can
help. But can I convince this grumpy cowboy to
finally claim me?

Courage County Fire & Rescue

The Firefighter's Curvy Nanny

As a single dad firefighter, I was only looking for a
quick fling. Then the curvy woman from last night
shows up. Turns out, she's my new nanny.

The Firefighter's Secret Baby

After a scorching one-night stand with a sexy
firefighter, I realize I'm pregnant...with my brother's
best friend's baby.

The Firefighter's Forbidden Fling

I knew a one night stand with my grumpy boss
wasn't the best idea...but I didn't think it would lead
to anything serious. I definitely didn't think it would
lead to a surprise pregnancy with this sexy firefighter.

GET A FREE COWBOY ROMANCE

Get Her Grumpy Cowboy for FREE:
https://www.MiaBrody.com/free-cowboy/

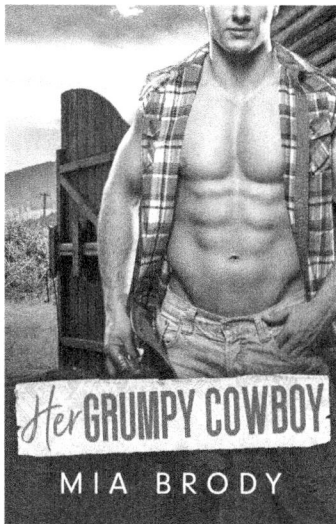

LIKE THIS STORY?

If you enjoyed this story, please post a review about it. Share what you liked or didn't like. It may not seem like much, but reviews are so important for indie authors like me who don't have the backing of a big publishing house.

Of course, you can also share your thoughts with me via email if you'd prefer to reach out that way. My email address is mia @ miabrody.com (remove the spaces). I love hearing from my readers!

ABOUT THE AUTHOR

Mia Brody writes steamy stories about alpha men who fall in love with big, beautiful women. She loves happy endings and every couple she writes will get one!

When she's not writing, Mia is searching for the perfect slice of cheesecake and reading books by her favorite instalove authors.

Keep in touch when you sign up for her newsletter: https://www.MiaBrody.com/news. It's the fastest way to hear about her new releases so you never miss one!

Printed in Dunstable, United Kingdom

68753952R00082